TOPAZ TAKES
A CHANCE

Helen Bailey

Illustrated by Bill Dare

First published in 2005 by
Hodder Children's Books
This Large Print edition published by
BBC Audiobooks
by arrangement with
Hodder Children's Books 2008

ISBN: 978 1405 662406

Bailey, Helen (

Topaz takes a
chance / Helen
Bailey ;
JLP

1712846

British Library Cataloguing in Publication Data available

Printed and bound in Great Britain by
Antony Rowe Ltd., Chippenham, Wiltshire

For Seren and Timur.

Turkish delight!

Limited Time - 2 Days Only!

SATURDAY – SUNDAY (STORE CLOSED SUNDAY)

20% OFF

PEACHY PORES PULL-OFF MASK

From Fruit Face Products

Bring this coupon to any branch of Wellington's The Chemist and see how **Peachy Pores** can give you a complexion like a furry peach!

Limit One coupon per customer; excludes all sizes other than Mega 3 litre size; offer expired yesterday.

✂ CUT ALONG DOTTED LINE

CHAPTER ONE

Filing into the school hall for assembly on the first day of the new term, Topaz looked around, gave Sapphire a mischievous grin and whispered excitedly, 'I'm going straight to Miss D's office after assembly, and I'm going to come right out with it!'

'Come out with what?' asked Sapphire.

'My plan to be a star!' said Topaz. 'I'm just going to take a deep breath and say, "Miss Diamond, I'm *so* not into school. This term, can I skip normal lessons and just concentrate on getting parts in adverts?"'

Sapphire Stratton stared at her friend in disbelief. Topaz was impatient to be a star and had been thinking of ways to become famous since they started at stage school last term. But today's plan was doomed from the start.

'Topaz L'Amour, you can't!' said Sapphire. 'Miss Diamond will go mad!

It's against school rules!'

Topaz hadn't forgotten that one of the rules for first-years at Precious Gems Stage School was that they couldn't appear in adverts, but she was hoping that she could persuade the Headmistress, Miss Diamond, to make an exception for her.

'If Rhapsody's Theatre Academy let their pupils be in adverts, I don't see why we can't!' she said indignantly. 'Octavia Quaver does adverts.'

Sapphire snorted and tossed her long blonde hair. 'I can't believe you want to be like that vile Rhapsody girl,' she said. 'In fact, I can't believe you want to be like *any* Rhapsody girl.'

Topaz's skin prickled at the thought that Sapphire might think she wanted to be like Octavia. Precious Gems Stage School and Rhapsody's Theatre Academy were bitter rivals. The girls from Rhapsody's were real stage-school brats, full of themselves and their own self-importance. It wasn't just a rumour that a Rhapsody's girl would stop at *nothing* to get a part. At the audition for Precious Gems,

Octavia had stolen Topaz's audition number so she could leave early to record 'burps' for a Slurp 'n' Burp fizzy drinks commercial. But it was something Octavia had said to Topaz when they appeared on the game show *Proof of the Pudding* that had stuck in her mind.

'I *chose* to go to Rhapsody's,' she had snarled, her blonde curls quivering with indignation at Topaz's suggestion that Precious Gems hadn't offered her a place. 'Pupils from Rhapsody's get *loads* of work.'

To make matters worse, every time Topaz switched on the radio the sound of the Slurp 'n' Burp advert filled the room.

'YOU GET BRILLIANT BURPS WITH SLURP 'N' BURP!' gushed the voice-over, after which Octavia let out a series of deep burps and finished by smacking her lips. Even Octavia's burps sounded bitchy.

'I'm just saying that if *she* can appear in ads, it can't be *that* difficult to get a part. How much talent does it take to burp?' Topaz let out a loud, deep burp and a pupil in front turned round in surprise. Topaz beamed back.

'Oh p–leese . . .' groaned Sapphire, sticking her tongue out in disgust. 'That's just gross. I don't know what's worse. Octavia, or you pretending to be Octavia.'

The hall was almost full and there was an air of restlessness as the pupils waited for the Headmistress to arrive. Even though there hadn't been any meals served in the school hall over the holidays, it still smelt of stale school dinners and dust. It *always* smelt of stinky food. As well as holding assemblies and school dinners, the hall doubled as the school theatre so that even when the school put on concerts and plays, the first thing the audience did on entering the room was wrinkle their noses at the smell.

'Have you seen Ruby?' asked Topaz, peering over heads and between bodies to try and catch a glimpse of their friend.

Sapphire shook her head. 'I know she was really nervous about playing the piano in assembly this morning. I'd

4

have liked to wish her good luck before the performance.'

Topaz turned round and noticed one of the teachers shutting the doors to the hall. Everyone was ready for the first assembly of the new term at Precious Gems. But where was Ruby Ruddle?

*   *   *

Hiding behind the blue curtains that covered the gym equipment lining one wall of the hall, Ruby wrung her sweaty hands in nervous despair. She'd hardly slept and had been worried ever since the moment at the end of last term when Miss Diamond had suggested she play the piano in assembly. Miss Diamond thought it would help her stage fright, but Ruby was so frightened she couldn't even *imagine* getting on to the stage. What was she going to do now? The last time she had been due to perform she had got herself in such a state, her father had had to buy up all the tickets for her concert. She'd felt pretty silly sitting in the church hall in Sutton Perry performing in front of just her mum, dad and brother.

Unless she let the fire alarm off or somehow got the sprinkler system to work, there didn't seem any way out now. Perhaps she could pretend to be ill? She'd used that excuse lots of times before, but Miss Diamond would just get her to perform another day. If only she could be like Topaz who loved being the centre of attention, or Sapphire, who didn't, but was used to it because of her film-star mother.

Ruby peered out from behind the curtain and her head swam. Had the school tripled in size? There seemed far more people out there than she remembered. And the piano! Usually it was hidden in the small orchestra pit under the stage, but it had been moved on to the stage, its walnut case looking as smooth as glass under the spotlight.

*   *   *

Miss Adelaide Diamond, one-time star of stage and screen, Headmistress of

6

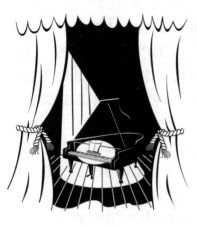

the school and five times Golden Nugget award-winner, swept through the crowd of pupils like a galleon in full sail, a whirl of flowing fabric, row upon row of amber beads bouncing around her ample bosom. Gliding up the steps and on to the stage (framed by the thick velvet curtains held back by gold rope), she stood in the spotlight, waiting for her audience to settle down. Not everything settled down quickly. It never failed to amaze the pupils that long after Miss Diamond had stopped moving, the beads around her neck continued to clack and quiver as if they were giving her a round of applause.

Topaz found it difficult to concentrate on anything Miss Diamond was saying. She was still working out the best way to ask permission to audition for adverts. Sapphire was thinking about whether her mother might come home at Easter—or whether she'd spend the holidays, yet again, on some exotic film set. Behind the curtain stood Ruby, pale, shaking and sweating.

All too quickly, Miss Diamond announced, 'As a change, Ruby Ruddle, one of our first-years, is going to play a short piece on the piano.'

Even though most of the school knew Ruby Ruddle only as the girl who had fallen off the stage at the auditions and landed on an upright oboe, everyone clapped and cheered. Even if it wasn't for them, stage-school pupils loved the sound of applause.

Ruby remained behind the curtain, shaking. People started peering around, wondering why they were clapping when there was no one to be seen. Miss Diamond spotted a pair of shoes sticking out from underneath the quivering curtain and called Ruby out. There was no turning back.

With stiff, painful steps Ruby made her way to the stage. Her legs felt like jelly and her head was swimming. The piano seemed as if it was at the end of a long tunnel. Somehow, she found herself climbing up the steps to the stage. It felt as if she was climbing a mountain. Feeling dizzy, she grabbed the handrail but her hands were so sweaty they slipped and she slid back down the stairs, landing in a crumpled heap at the bottom, still holding the rail like a limp rag doll, her sheet music fluttering around her. Miss Diamond hurried to her rescue, gathered up her music and hauled her on to the stage. She was beginning to wonder whether asking Ruby to perform had been a good idea after all.

'What are you going to play for us today?' she asked a terrified Ruby.

Ruby mumbled something under her breath.

'I don't think the back row quite caught that,' said Miss Diamond.

' "The Entertainer",' stammered Ruby through a row of gritted teeth.

Miss Diamond turned Ruby around by her shoulders and pointed her towards the piano. Ruby walked to the stool as if she was a robot and sat rigidly. Her cheeks were burning, her hands were shaking and even her bright red plaits seemed to quiver with nerves. The school was silent except for the sound of Ruby's knees knocking together. People began to give embarrassed coughs and shift their feet uncomfortably. Topaz and Sapphire looked at each other in despair. Their friend was frozen with fear in front of the entire school and no one seemed to know what to do. Ruby sat at the piano, motionless, unable even to lift the lid.

I've got to help her! thought Topaz. She pushed her way through the crowd to the front of the hall.

Clambering on to the stage, she noticed Miss Diamond looking surprised, then relieved.

What is *Topaz up to?* Adelaide Diamond wondered.

' "The Entertainer" is *so* much better with a dance routine, don't you think?' Topaz announced to the school, as she casually flipped up the lid of the baby grand and smiled at her wide-eyed audience. The pupil in front of them might not have had any formal training until she came to stage school, but just as she had done at the auditions, Topaz lit up the stage and captured her audience in the way most actresses could only dream of. She felt more at home on the stage than off it. When she stepped on stage she wasn't just a girl from a tiny top-floor flat in Andromeda Road in one of the poorer parts of Starbridge. On stage, real life stayed the other side of the footlights. It didn't matter where you lived, how much money you had or whether you had the right blazer. You could be anything you wanted to be, and Topaz wanted to be a star.

'Take it away, Ruby!' cried Topaz.

At first, Ruby began to play slowly, but within a couple of bars her fingers were running up and down the keys whilst Topaz danced around the piano, waving an imaginary top hat and cane, tap-dancing with no tapping sounds but having the time of her life. As Ruby came to the end of the piece, Topaz shouted to the audience, 'An encore— and now it's *your* turn!' and Ruby played again, this time with the entire school clapping and dancing. There had never been a school assembly like it.

Thank goodness she didn't apply to Rhapsody's, thought Miss Diamond as Topaz threw herself across the piano at the end to rapturous applause.

CHAPTER TWO

Miss Diamond opened the door to her study and Topaz followed her in.

'Just give me a moment,' she said, going over to her desk and shuffling some papers.

Topaz loved looking around Miss Diamond's office. More like a theatre dressing room than a headmistress' study, every inch of it oozed show business and glamour. Fixed to one wall was a huge mirror, the edge studded with soft pink lights. A large glass cabinet crammed with awards and trophies of every kind ran behind Miss Diamond's desk, her five Golden Nugget awards standing to attention at the front. Topaz smiled as she noticed her own award, the Golden Whisk she'd won on *Proof of the Pudding*. Dotted around the room were framed newspaper articles, posters, glowing reviews and pictures of a young Adelaide Diamond at parties and opening nights surrounded by glamorous show business friends.

Miss Diamond looked up from her desk and said, 'Now, Topaz, what was it you wanted to see me for? If it's about what just happened in assembly . . .'

Topaz fiddled nervously with her watchstrap and blurted out, 'There's something I'd like to discuss with you. I need your help.'

Adelaide Diamond looked fondly at the anxious first-year standing in front of her. The first term at stage school hadn't been easy for Topaz. She'd had plenty of talent and enthusiasm but no theatrical training before she auditioned for the school, so there had been extra classes in dance and music after school to bring her up to the standard of the other first-years. Adelaide knew that even though the scholarship paid for Topaz's school fees, money was tight for Topaz's mother.

And Topaz wasn't popular with *all* the teachers. Some of them had pointed out that Topaz spent more time dreaming of becoming a star than doing academic lessons, but as far as stage work was concerned, Topaz had done everything that was asked of her and had come through with flying colours.

Miss Diamond moved to one of the overstuffed red velvet sofas and gestured towards the other. 'Come and sit down and tell me how I can help,' she said gently.

Topaz hesitated. Every time she sat on that sofa it seemed to have a life of its own. Either the springs pinged and pinched her bottom or the pile of cushions she sat on to avoid the springs toppled over. One way or another, that sofa had it in for her. Miss Diamond nodded again towards the sofa and Topaz carefully lowered herself on to the grasping velvet upholstery, perching nervously on the edge.

She was just about to launch into her speech when the telephone rang and Miss Diamond moved to her desk to answer it. Her voice had a sharp edge.

'Tell her I'm not in,' she barked into the receiver. 'If she rings again, tell her the same thing.'

Miss Diamond put the phone down with a bang, smoothed her hair and sat back down.

'I'm sorry,' she said, seeming a little flustered. 'Now, what were we talking about?'

It was Topaz's big chance to impress Miss Diamond and convince her of her plan to get into adverts. She sat up straight, took a deep breath and announced, 'Miss Diamond, I'm *so* not into school, and this term I'd like to skip normal lessons and just concentrate on getting parts in adverts. Like the Rhapsody girls.'

Adelaide Diamond's finely pencilled eyebrows shot up into her hairline and her back stiffened. The beads around her neck began to quiver. One of the first warnings the senior pupils had given the juniors was that the size of the swell of Miss Diamond's chest was directly proportional to the trouble you were in. Seeing Miss Diamond's chest rise and fall like a heavy sea, Topaz knew a tidal wave was about to break.

Suddenly there was a bang, a crash, then the door of the office burst open, and a small white-faced woman smelling of stale cigarettes hurtled into the office, brandishing a mobile phone. The springs in the sofa burst into life and with an almighty *ping!*, propelled Topaz off the edge and on to the floor just as Adelaide Diamond jumped to her feet.

'Ha!' the woman yelled at Miss Diamond, 'I *knew* you were in!'

'I'd like you to leave,' Miss Diamond said to the woman in an icy voice. 'I'd like you to leave NOW!'

The woman made no effort to move but stood with her arms folded across her chest. 'I'd like *you* to return my telephone calls,' she said in a gravelly voice. 'We've business to discuss.'

'I have *nothing* to say to you, Zelma Flint!' proclaimed Miss Diamond, marching to the door and holding it open. 'Nothing!'

No one seemed to notice Topaz crouching on her knees at the foot of the sofa and Topaz herself didn't dare move.

The woman marched over to Miss Diamond's desk, pushed some papers out of the way and leant against the edge. *'I'm* not going anywhere until we discuss that girl of yours. At least hear me out.'

Adelaide Diamond knew just how persistent Zelma Flint could be. Zelma was as hungry for a deal now as she had been all those years ago when she was Adelaide's agent. She'd been ignoring Zelma's telephone calls but she should have known she'd never give up. She'd stay in Adelaide's office all day and all night if she had to. Zelma was like a hound following a scent. She had talent in her sights and she knew a star when she saw one. Zelma was after Topaz. But where *was* Topaz?

'Topaz?' Adelaide called out.

'I'm here!' Topaz replied from the carpet.

Zelma Flint rushed to the sofa, held

out a gnarled nicotine-stained hand and pulled Topaz to her feet. 'I'm Zelma Flint, Starbridge's *top* celebrity agent,' she said, smiling to reveal a row of teeth like little yellow pegs. 'You're the reason I'm here! I saw you on *Proof of the Pudding* and in the Starbridge Christmas Show. I've got a very interesting proposition for you.'

Miss Diamond looked flustered. The beads around her neck were quivering frantically.

'Topaz, will you please go. We'll continue our conversation another time.'

Topaz stood between the two women, her eyes as wide as saucers. Her mind was racing. Could it really be true what she had heard? Zelma Flint had been trying to contact Miss Diamond about her? Why hadn't Miss Diamond told her? What was the interesting proposition? Why did

19

Miss Diamond dislike Zelma Flint? It couldn't just be that she smelt of horrid cigarettes and had yellow teeth and fingers. Why didn't Miss Diamond return Zelma's calls?

'Topaz!' Miss Diamond barked, causing Topaz to jump. 'I've asked you to leave!'

As Topaz moved towards the door, Zelma leapt in front of her and pushed her business card into Topaz's hand. 'Just so you'll always know where to find me,' she said, giving Adelaide Diamond a triumphant look. '*I* could make *you* a star!'

*　　　*　　　*

'Giving Topaz your card was a low trick, even for you,' said Adelaide, sitting behind her desk, staring at Zelma Flint. 'You shouldn't have burst in like that. You're out of order, Zelma.'

Zelma gave a dismissive shrug. 'You wouldn't return my calls. You wouldn't see me. What else was I supposed to do?'

Adelaide threw Zelma a sharp look. 'You *ruined* my career,' she said. 'I'm not about to let you do the same to Topaz.'

'I'm not here to pick over the bones of your career,' said Zelma. 'Topaz has talent. I saw her on that game show and at the theatre and she *oozed* star quality. The stage loves her, the camera loves her. I look at her and I see a star!'

'You look at her and you see money,' flashed Adelaide. 'Her career needs careful handling. She's very young.'

'Young *and* ambitious,' retorted Zelma. 'You can't keep a good star down and you of all people should know that!' She jabbed a nicotine-stained finger at Adelaide. 'What are you going to do? Keep her in cotton wool until Rhapsody's comes along and offers her a place at stage school *and* paid work?'

Adelaide stood up and turned her back on Zelma. She needed time to think. Topaz had already mentioned the girls at Rhapsody's getting adverts, even in the junior years.

'And what makes you think you are the right person?' asked Adelaide, turning back to face Zelma. 'Better the devil you know than the devil you don't?'

'Contacts,' said Zelma. 'You may not like me and you no longer trust me, but even *you* have to admit no one else in Starbridge has an address book like mine!'

Adelaide sat back down at her desk and rubbed her eyes. Zelma wasn't going to give up without a fight. It was only a matter of time before other agents came knocking at her door, asking to represent Topaz. Some wouldn't even ask. They'd go straight to Topaz behind her back.

'What do you have in mind?' she asked.

Zelma Flint saw her opportunity and gave Adelaide an oily yellow smile. She perched on the front of Adelaide's desk. 'For starters, I'm thinking a low-key regional print advert. Not too much exposure. The right product for her age group with limited press and only in targeted magazines. If I could find something like that, would you put Topaz forward for casting?'

Adelaide remained silent and Zelma looked pleased.

'As you haven't said no, I'll take that as a yes,' she said, rummaging in her bag. 'As luck would have it, I had a few drinks over Christmas with Petunia Bluff's husband Leo, from Bluff, Hype & Bluster advertising agency. He wondered if I had anyone suitable for this campaign.'

She pulled a crumpled piece of paper out of her bag, blew ash off it and handed it to Adelaide.

'Perfect, isn't it?' cried Zelma, clapping her hands. 'Just the right start!'

Adelaide shook her head and pushed the paper back towards Zelma. 'We have a rule that first-years can't be in adverts,' she said.

Zelma banged the desk. 'Who makes the rules?' she demanded, her eyes flashing.

'I do,' answered Adelaide.

'Then rewrite them!' bellowed Zelma.

Adelaide thought for a moment. It *was* a good opportunity. Small enough not to interfere with schoolwork, but just enough to keep Topaz from thinking about Rhapsody's.

'I can't send only Topaz to the casting,' she said. 'I can't rewrite the rules for one pupil. I'll have to arrange for the whole class to go to the casting and Topaz will just have to take her chance with everyone else.'

'Are you mad?' rasped Zelma. 'I can't tell Leo Bluff that twenty people are going to turn up. Three—three at the most.'

'Three it is, then,' said Adelaide, walking Zelma to the door. She looked Zelma straight in the eye and said menacingly, 'Let Topaz down and I'll make sure you never work in this town *ever* again.'

Zelma gave a throaty chuckle. 'Don't worry,' she said. 'I can't make you a star any longer, but I've got big plans for Topaz. I can't wait to see her face when you tell her!'

They didn't have to wait long, for as Adelaide went to open the door there was an almighty yell. Topaz, who had been listening through the keyhole, found her hair had become wrapped around the door handle and fell into the room.

CHAPTER THREE

'A zit advert!' exploded Topaz. 'How can I be a star in a Zit Stop! advert? No one mentioned anything about me being in a zit advert!'

Ruby gave Topaz a sharp look. 'What you do you mean, *me*?' she asked. 'Any of us could be in this advert!'

Topaz didn't answer but studied the piece of paper they had all been given, and groaned.

'The slogan is going to be "Don't Pop It—Stop It!". How much worse can this get?'

She tossed the piece of paper away. She'd been thinking for days about what sort of advert Zelma Flint had arranged for her. Holiday adverts on sun-drenched beaches; hair adverts for glossy straight hair that she would flick about her shoulders in a halo of sunlight; chocolate adverts where she could eat a bar of chocolate *and* get paid for it. So many possibilities! It had *never* occurred to her that the advert would be for spot cream!

'At least you *want* to be in it,' said Ruby bitterly. 'I can't think of anything worse. Miss Diamond said she was putting me forward for the experience. Since when did a musician need to be in a spot advert?'

Ruby had thought about not telling her parents at all, but Miss Diamond had rung Ruby's mother and explained the situation. The audition would be good experience for Ruby, particularly after her disastrous assembly.

Sapphire was sitting quietly flicking through her copy of *Hot Science!* magazine.

'I'm amazed that Miss Diamond is letting *any* of us go to the casting,' she said. 'What about the school rule that no first-years can be in adverts?' She looked up at Topaz with suspicious eyes. 'How *did* you persuade her?'

Topaz shifted uncomfortably in her seat. She was desperate to tell the others that she'd met Zelma Flint and that Zelma wanted to make her a star, but it sounded big-headed, so she just shrugged and said, 'I just said what I told you I'd say.'

'And Miss Diamond said OK, just like that?' asked Ruby.

Topaz nodded.

Ruby was still unhappy. She was already getting herself into a state at the thought of the casting and the possibility that she might get the part. She had loads of freckles but no spots. She was a good advert for Zit Stop!

'Why do all of us need to go?' she said. 'It was your idea, not ours!' She turned to Sapphire. 'It's all right for you, you're used to the celebrity lifestyle.'

Sapphire sighed, looked up from *Hot Science!* and said calmly, 'I'm not allowed to go.'

'What!' exclaimed Topaz. 'Sapphi, why?'

'My mother has put her stiletto down and said I can't go.'

'Is it because it's a spot advert?' asked Ruby. 'Isn't it glam enough?'

'It's *any* advert,' Sapphire replied. 'She didn't know it was a spot advert when I asked her.'

Topaz was astonished. Why on earth would a famous film star like Vanessa Stratton object to an advert?

'I thought she was desperate for you to be in show business,' she said.

Sapphire shrugged. 'She doesn't think of adverts as show business, I guess,' she said, thinking back to the last conversation she'd had with her mother.

*   *   *

Lounging on a sun bed beside a pool fringed by palm trees, Vanessa Stratton had almost choked on her champagne

29

cocktail when her daughter telephoned to tell her about the casting.

'Don't even bother sending Rupert the release form to sign,' she spluttered. 'I am *not* having my daughter appearing in tawdry little regional ads. Darling, Strattons don't *do* regional.'

Sapphire didn't particularly want to go to the casting, but neither did she want the consequences of not going. If she told Miss Diamond she couldn't go, Miss D would telephone her mother who would ask what on earth did she think she was doing, putting a Stratton forward for such a little ad? Sapphire would be called to Miss Diamond's office and told that it would be better if she didn't go. Then everyone would sneer and say, 'Ooh, that Stratton girl thinks she's above being in little adverts just because her mum is a film star.'

'Please, Mum,' Sapphire pleaded. 'There's no guarantee I'll be chosen and it'll be good experience. After what I said when you didn't come home for Christmas, I thought you'd be pleased.'

At the other end of the phone, Venessa clicked her fingers, pointed at her empty champagne glass and waited for it to be refilled. Sometimes Sapphire could be *so* awkward, and she could feel this was building into a two-champagne-cocktail type of conversation.

'You do remember what I said, don't you?' asked Sapphire.

Silence crackled down the phone.

More champagne arrived and Vanessa took a gulp.

'Of course I do, darling. You said you wanted to be a doctor, not an actress. But Daddy and I didn't take it seriously. You were just upset that we weren't home for Christmas, again.'

Sapphire's heart leapt. So her father knew she hadn't wanted to go to stage school and follow the rest of the family into show business. Perhaps he had stood up for her after all!

'You told Daddy? When? What did he say? Has he finished directing that film?'

Vanessa stretched back on her sun bed and wriggled her toes. There was a small chip in the nail polish on her left big toe.

I must get that fixed as soon as I'm off the phone, she thought to herself. *Snapped!*, the celebrity magazine, were due to feature her in a photo shoot later that day.

'Mum!' prompted Sapphire. 'What did Dad say?'

Vanessa took another gulp of champagne.

'Sinclair agreed with me. He said if you want to be a doctor, why not get a part playing one? You get to wear a nice white coat and stride around saving lives without spending years training!'

Sapphire groaned. Sometimes, she couldn't believe her parents really *were* her parents. Perhaps she had been found by the stage door as a baby? That would explain a lot of things.

'So, can I go to this casting or not?' she asked.

Vanessa Stratton was firm. 'Absolutely not, darling. If you really have your little heart set on being in an advert, I'll arrange for you do something much more high profile without any need to audition.'

'Mum, that's not the point!' protested Sapphire. 'I *want* to be like everyone else. I don't want favours. Whatever I do, I want to make it on my own!'

'Of course it's the point,' said Vanessa, irritated. 'What on earth is the point of knowing people if you can't use them?'

There was silence. Sapphire didn't know what else to say. As far as her mother was concerned, the matter was closed.

*   *   *

Sapphire sighed as she finished telling Ruby and Topaz about the poolside conversation, leaving out the bit where her mum had called the advert 'tawdry'.

'Wish *my* mum wouldn't let me go,' grumbled Ruby. 'I'd give *anything* to get out of it.'

'Do you really want to go?' Topaz asked Sapphire.

Sapphire sighed again. 'I didn't,' she said, 'but now Mum says I can't, I do. I really want to do something that doesn't rely on the Stratton name.'

'So go!' said Topaz. 'If your mum's abroad, she'll never know.'

'What if I get the part?' asked Sapphire. 'How I am going to explain that?'

Remembering the conversation between Miss Diamond and Zelma Flint she'd heard through the keyhole, Topaz said a little too quickly, 'You won't!' before adding, 'I mean, you probably won't.'

'What about this?' said Sapphire, fishing the release form out of her bag. 'Miss Diamond won't let me go without it.'

Topaz couldn't believe a little thing like a signature could stop you from doing something you really wanted. When she had auditioned for Precious Gems she'd forged her mum's signature on the form, and when she'd been at Starbridge Middle she was forever writing letters from her mum, excusing her from games.

'So, forge her signature,' said Topaz with a shrug. 'I used to do it all the time.'

Ruby looked shocked. 'You can't do that!' she said. 'It's illegal.'

'It's not against the law!' said Topaz, not really sure whether it was or not. 'It's just a little white lie.'

'I can't,' said Sapphire. 'I don't know what my mother's signature looks like. I've never seen her handwriting.'

Ruby and Topaz stared at Sapphire in shocked disbelief. How could you not recognize your own mother's handwriting?

Sapphire saw the expression on her friends' faces and looked embarrassed.

'I mean, I know she does a sort of huge V with a kiss next to it when she signs autographs, but that's not really her signature. I'm not sure if that would count for the form.'

Topaz thought about her own signature. She spent hours practising Topaz L'Am♥ur, but perhaps T♥ might be better. She'd try it a few

35

times to see how it looked.

'But what about birthdays?' asked Ruby. 'Who signs your card?'

Sapphire shrugged, for a moment looked as if she might burst into tears, and began to wind her long blonde hair around one finger.

'Her assistant, Rupert, signs and sends them for her. Either that or . . . Miss Bean.' Sapphire blushed. She'd been about to say 'Nanny Bean' but felt too old to admit that her childhood nanny still looked after her, even if it was just because her mother and father were never at home.

'So forge the Bean woman's signature,' said Topaz, who thought Sapphire was making a fuss over nothing.

'I can't get her into trouble,' said Sapphire. 'I don't want to go *that* badly!'

Topaz grabbed the form from Sapphire and scribbled a mark that looked as if a brick had been dropped on to a spider from a great height.

'There!' she said, handing it back to an astonished Sapphire. 'If you don't know your mum's signature, Miss D certainly won't.'

CHAPTER FOUR

The weeks between meeting Zelma Flint and the day of the Zit Stop! casting seemed to stretch for ever.

Ruby hadn't managed to persuade her parents that it was demeaning for a budding musician to appear in an advert for spot cream, and was having nightmares about somehow getting the part and finding her face plastered across magazines next to photo love stories.

Sapphire was worried that *she* would get the part and would have to explain to her mother why she had gone behind her back.

Topaz, after talking to one of the

senior pupils, Pearl Wong, was excited about the casting.

'*Everyone* has to start *somewhere,*' Pearl had said when Topaz had told her of her disappointment that it wasn't a more glamorous advert. 'Name any famous actress and I bet you they've done some *really* dodgy commercials in the past.'

Pearl knew what she was talking about. She was 'Girl Eating Burger' in one of the Speedy Snax commercials, and the only person Topaz had ever met who had been in an advert.

So Topaz sat in class, practising her autograph, planning what she might buy with the fee she would get from the advert and dreaming of the day when she would be interviewed and could purr, 'Well, my big break came when I was spotted in a spot advert!'

The fact that she hadn't actually *got* the part yet didn't worry her. Having overheard Zelma Flint talking to Miss Diamond, she was sure that the casting was only a formality. The advert was hers! Zelma would make *sure* she became a star.

Not everyone at Precious Gems thought sending first-years to a casting was a good idea, and there were dark mutterings of discontent in the staff room. What had prompted Adelaide Diamond to change the rules? They could understand her sending Sapphire Stratton, but why Topaz L'Amour? Several teachers had already complained that Topaz already spent far too much time dreaming of becoming a star at the expense of her schoolwork.

So, during chemistry practical, Miss Tuffstone, the science teacher, was surprised to see Topaz crouching at the bench staring intently at a roaring Bunsen burner. It was the first time Topaz had shown the slightest enthusiasm for chemistry.

'How nice to see you showing such an interest,' Miss Tuffstone said. 'Have you noticed something unusual that you'd like to share with the class?'

Topaz looked up at the teacher, her eyes wide behind the safety goggles.

'I'm just trying to decide whether I photograph better from the left or right side,' she said, looking at her reflection in the stem of the burner. 'What do you think?'

Topaz had tried to pretend her remark was a joke, which it wasn't, but Miss Tuffstone, whom the class nicknamed Miss Toadstone because of her bulging eyes and double chin, didn't believe her and had demanded she came back after school for double detention.

*   *   *

As she hurried down the corridor after detention, Topaz could hear the clatter of heavy feet jumping up and down in the PT ballet class. PTs were 'part timers' who came to classes at Precious Gems after their own school had finished. It didn't matter if you had a voice like a foghorn or danced with two left feet. As long as you could afford the fees you could join a class. Most of the full-time pupils at Precious Gems looked down on the PTs and thought them 'tragic', but Topaz was secretly grateful to them. Not only did their fees pay for her scholarship, but she'd also been in several PT classes for extra tuition when she'd first joined Precious Gems. The classes had been hard work but they'd been fun.

A PT girl she recognized from last term came rushing down the corridor, late for her class.

'Hi, Topaz!' she gasped as she approached. 'You look pleased with yourself!'

'I'm going to be in an advert tomorrow,' beamed Topaz.

'Cool!' yelled the girl over her shoulder as she rushed past.

Yes, it is *cool!* thought Topaz, skipping down the steps of the school. In a few hours' time she would be well on her way to commercial stardom. Nothing could stop her now!

*   *   *

On her way home, Topaz popped into Wellington's the Chemist to get some proper shampoo so that her hair would look gorgeous for the casting. Not the stuff her mum bought from The

Bargain Basket which said 'Economy' and came in huge bottles, but something which had words like 'smooth', 'silky' and 'added bi-vitamin X3' on the bottle and was advertised on the telly by girls with long shiny hair which they tossed about their shoulders in sunlit slow motion.

As she was looking at the vast array of bottles on the shelf and trying to decide whether her hair was 'rebellious' or just simply 'unmanageable', a girl appeared alongside her wearing a badge saying, 'Want Perfect Pores? Ask Me How!'

'Hello!' said the girl, flashing a bright white smile. 'My name is Poppy and I'd like to introduce you to Peachy Pores. The pull-off mask that reveals a peachy, soft complexion and perfect pores in one easy step.'

Topaz wasn't sure why anyone would want a face like a hairy peach, but Poppy certainly had lovely skin.

Poppy handed Topaz a small sachet. 'Here's a sample. If you bring back the packet within the next week, you can get twenty per cent off a full-size product,' she gushed, before moving off down the aisle.

For the same price as her mum's economy shampoo, Topaz bought a tiny bottle of Fabulous Follicles which promised instantly smooth, sleek hair, and left the shop. In the background Poppy continued to trill, 'Hello! My name is Poppy and I'd like to introduce you to Peachy Pores!'

*   *   *

Throwing her bag down in the tiny hallway of the top-floor flat she and her mother shared in Andromeda Road, Topaz wandered through into the kitchen. There was a note on the fridge from her mum saying, 'T in Oven'. Almost every evening her mother would be out cleaning houses and offices, just to keep Topaz in tutus and tap-shoes. Money was still *very* tight. Despite her mother's promise of a new blazer for Christmas, Topaz had started the new term still wearing an old maroon hand-me-down instead of the claret one on the Precious Gems

44

uniform list. Topaz knew her mum did the best she could and she shuddered when she thought of the fuss she'd made at having to start at Precious Gems wearing a second-hand boy's blazer, because there was no money to buy a new one.

She opened the oven door and pulled out a plate, wrinkling her nose at what had been mince and potatoes but was now just a grey, greasy sludge. Her mum wasn't to know nasty Miss Toadstone had given her double detention and that Topaz had made a detour to Wellington's. Her tea had obviously been festering in the oven for hours.

She put the plate in the microwave, set the timer and peered through the glass. She must remember to keep an eye on her plate or she'd be spending the evening picking bits off the walls of the microwave. She'd had several disasters with food exploding in the microwave, and had decided it was better to spend a few minutes watching it through the glass door, than an hour cleaning up the kitchen.

As she watched the mince begin to bubble around the edge of the plate, she caught sight of herself in the glass door. Was that a swelling on her cheek? She peered closer and poked at her skin. It was definitely something. She poked again. It seemed even more swollen than before. An underground zit! A zit which had been sitting there for days just waiting for its opportunity to erupt the night before her big break in advertising!

On Topaz's three-level disaster scale, this definitely counted as a disastrophe. The 3D-scale covered minor problems, classed as 'disasterettes', major problems which were ranked as straightforward disasters and finally, the worst possible disaster in the worst possible context, with catastrophic consequences for life. In other words, a 'disastrophe'.

Take this spot.

If this spot had appeared weeks ago and had now gone, leaving just a red mark which could be covered by slapping on plenty of blemish B gone cover-up in Bare Beige, this would only be classed as a minor annoyance, a disasterette. Even if the people at the Zit Stop! casting noticed the thick layer of cover-up, they'd realize the spot had gone and their product had worked. If the spot had appeared a week ago and was still a bit swollen, that would be a disaster because it would still be lumpy and look as if she hadn't been using Zit Stop!—but by putting on even *more* layers of cover-up, there was just a slim chance that the Zit Stop! people might think, 'Ah, that zit is on its way down. Our product has worked.' But to go to a Zit Stop! casting with a zit which threatened to burst through even the thickest layer of cover-up and sit flashing like a red beacon on your cheek on the *very* morning that you were auditioning for a product which was supposed to *stop* spots, was quite definitely a full scale disastrophe. She'd never be the star of the Zit Stop!

advert if she had a zit. If they chose someone with a zit, it was obvious the product didn't work! What *was* she going to do? Suddenly, Topaz remembered Poppy with the Peachy Pores, ran into the hall and dug the sachet out of her bag. This was exactly what she needed!

Rushing into the bathroom, she crammed her hair under her mother's flowery bath hat, ripped open the sachet of Peachy Pores and slapped the cool pale pink goo on her face. *Then* she looked at the instructions: 'Smooth over a wet face for five to ten minutes, depending on the severity of the problem.'

Topaz felt she had a severe problem. What could be more severe than a zit threatening to explode the day before a photo shoot? Ten minutes didn't seem nearly long enough. She'd try it for twenty minutes or maybe even thirty. And surely it didn't matter that her face had been dry when she put the mask on, even though the instructions said it must be wet? She wandered into her bedroom, lay back on her bed and smiled. Tomorrow she would be a star.

*   *   *

The shrieks from the top-floor flat at number 14 Andromeda Road could be heard at the bus stop opposite.

'My daughter's had a little accident with a face mask,' said Topaz's mother, Lola, as she answered the door to the people in the flat below who had come up to see whether everything was all right.

Topaz had fallen asleep smothered in Peachy Pores and was only woken by the sound of her mother coming through the front door later that evening. The face mask had set solid and, as no amount of tugging or washing would get it off, Lola had to pick it off her daughter's face bit by painful bit with her eyebrow tweezers. For each bit of mask that came off, a bit of skin came with it, causing Topaz to shriek.

49

When her mother had finished picking off the Peachy Pores mask, Topaz looked in despair at her red face in the mirror. Hot tears stung as they rolled down her raw cheeks. She might not have any zits, but how could she be a star with a face like a boiled beetroot?

This really is *a disastrophe*, she thought miserably as she trudged into the kitchen to help her mother pick bits of forgotten mince off the inside of the microwave.

CHAPTER FIVE

Even though it was cold and damp, the girls were relieved that they were going to the casting on the bus with Pearl Wong, rather than in the school minibus with Miss Diamond. Miss Diamond was a *terrible* driver who took corners at high speed and paid no attention to stop signs. Often, pupils would arrive at an audition and stagger off the minibus with green faces and shaky legs, disappearing behind the nearest bush to be sick.

'*I'm* in the next Speedy Snax campaign,' Pearl said to Topaz as the bus rattled through Starbridge. 'I don't even have to audition. The director said I was so perfect, the part is mine.'

As Pearl continued to chatter on about Speedy Snax, Ruby nervously chewed the end of her plaits and thought about the casting, whilst Sapphire stared out of the window and thought about her mother. No one had noticed Topaz's red face. They were all too wrapped up in their own problems.

Topaz buried her face deep into her scarf and flicked through her copy of *Snapped!* magazine. One particular article caught her attention. She passed the magazine over her shoulder to Sapphire.

'Look!' she said, pointing at picture of a woman by a pool on a sun bed. 'There's your mum.'

Sapphire peered closely at the picture. The caption said, 'Vanessa on Vacation' and featured a double-page spread of Vanessa Stratton lying on a sun bed, sitting on a sun bed, standing behind a sun bed, but *always* holding a glass of champagne and surrounded by tanned, bare-chested men wearing tiny shorts.

'Mmm,' said Sapphire vaguely, as if

everyone saw their family holiday snaps in a magazine. 'So *that's* where she is.'

*   *   *

As the bus pulled up to the bus stop, Topaz noticed a group of girls in grey blazers hanging around the shelter. They were her old friends from Starbridge Middle who were now at Starbridge High. They weren't friends with her now she was at stage school, especially not Kylie Slate, who had stolen Topaz's best friend Janice Stone. Topaz saw Kylie leaning against the bus shelter, chewing gum, her face set in a permanent snarl. Did Kylie *ever* go to school? Topaz kept her head down hoping no one would recognize her. There was a jeer as they left the bus.

'Ooh! It's the PG girls,' sneered Kylie, spotting their Precious Gems blazers. 'They think they're pretty grand but we think they're pretty gross!'

The crowd laughed and someone lobbed an empty can of Slurp 'n' Burp in their direction.

'What horrid girls!' said Sapphire as they walked towards the studio. 'Who on earth would go to a school like that?'

Topaz shrugged. 'I've no idea,' she lied from behind her scarf.

*　　　*　　　*

Stopping outside a large redbrick building, Pearl Wong pushed a button labelled Studio 45.

'We're here for a casting,' Pearl called out into the crackling intercom.

The door was released and the girls trooped into the gloomy building.

In a dark, narrow corridor, at the top of a long flight of stairs, stood a girl with a clipboard and a Polaroid camera. Because of the Peachy Pores disaster the night before, Topaz hadn't had a chance to use the bottle of Fabulous Follicles shampoo, and her hair was springing out in all directions. She reached into her bag to grab her hairbrush, but before she had time to use it, clipboard girl had taken her picture, ripped the damp shot from the

54

camera and was fanning it and blowing on it at the same time. She stapled it to a form, handed it to Topaz and said, 'Fill this out and take it to the room along the corridor.'

Topaz looked in horror at her picture. A walk in the cold from the bus stop and the climb up several steep flights of stairs had done nothing to calm her red face. She looked like a surprised beetroot. In the background, she could hear the buzzer going and other Zit Stop! hopefuls trudging up the stairs and she felt a stab of disappointment. It hadn't occurred to her that there would be others here. From what she'd heard Zelma Flint say, the part was hers!

She walked along the gloomy corridor, pushed open a door on which was taped a piece of paper saying, 'Zit' and entered a vast room, white from floor to ceiling. Battered silver equipment cases and tangled cables littered the floor. A camera perched on a tripod stood to attention in front of a massive white umbrella—under which sat a small stool, lit on either side by

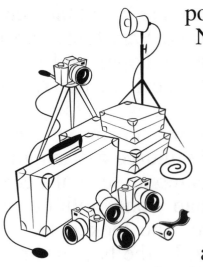

powerful spotlights. Nearby, a trolley was piled high with rolls of film, cameras and lenses.

Topaz crouched on one of the silver equipment cases and began to fill in her form. Name; Address; Date of Birth; Hair Colour; School/Agent. She began to scribble away. All the questions seemed straightforward until she got to 'Experience'. She stared at the empty space. Contestant on *Proof of the Pudding* didn't sound professional enough. Nor did 'back end of a horse in the Starbridge Christmas Show'. She chewed the end of her pen and looked round the room. It had begun to fill up with other girls. They were all writing away, filling out their forms, and seemed to have lots to say. Looking again at the blank space next to 'Experience' she wrote, 'Masses'. Next to 'School/Agent' she crossed out 'Precious Gems' and fished Zelma Flint's card from her purse, even though Miss Diamond had made it quite clear that Zelma wasn't Topaz's agent—not yet, anyway.

Having an agent will show I'm serious, she thought, copying out Zelma's details. *What harm can it do?*

* * *

A tall man strode into the studio followed by a small man dressed from head to toe in black and entirely bald, except for a tiny goatee beard.

'Welcome!' bellowed the tall man. 'I'm Leo Bluff from Bluff, Hype & Bluster and I'm here on behalf of my client, Zit Stop!, to oversee the photo shoot.'

He hesitated as if he were waiting for a round of applause, but getting no reaction, he carried on.

'We're *thrilled* to have the services of top photographer Lenny "The Lens" for this shoot—a true artist who has worked on many top campaigns including,' Leo gave a dramatic pause, 'the award-winning chip pan safety advert!'

There was a gasp. Leo beamed and turned to the little man behind him.

'I'm sure you don't mind me telling everyone that you lost your eyebrows on that shoot,' Leo added, turning back to the crowd of assorted hopefuls and their chaperones, 'which I think says a great deal about Lenny's dedication to his work.'

Lenny nodded as a murmur of approval rippled around the studio.

Leo beamed again. 'As you know, this is a cast *and* shoot. Time is tight. We'll call you over one by one and make a quick decision. Anything we need to change, we can do on the computer, later.'

In the background came the sound of a low thump followed by a high-pitched gasp. People looked at each other with puzzled expressions.

Thump. Gasp. Thump. Gasp. The sound came up the stairs, along the corridor and stopped for a moment before the door burst open and a woman in a shiny purple tracksuit screamed, 'Someone get my daughter a chair!'

Draped over the shoulder of a sweating and gasping Melody Sharp was none other than Octavia Quaver, her leg in plaster from toe to thigh.

'I sort of did that,' Topaz whispered to Ruby and Sapphire, as Octavia pushed Melody aside and collapsed into a nearby chair.

It was true. At the Starbridge Christmas Show, Octavia had been playing the front end of a pantomime horse and Topaz the back, but whilst arguing with Topaz, Octavia had forgotten she had a horse's nose, hit her head on an overhead beam and fallen down some stairs, breaking her leg.

Topaz was going to pretend she hadn't seen Octavia when she noticed the most wonderful thing. Octavia had a spot the size of a small town right on the end of her nose. A spot so large it could almost have its own postcode. There was *no way* that she would be chosen for a Zit Stop! advert. If they used Octavia it was obvious that the product was useless! Topaz smiled inside. Her face might be red from the Peachy Pores mask, but she didn't have a stonking great boil on the end of her nose! Perhaps this wasn't going to be such a disastrophe after all.

Octavia recognized Topaz. 'You!' she screeched, thrusting her plastered leg towards Topaz. '*You* did this to me!'

Octavia's mother stomped over, carrying a huge bag.

'Mum,' Octavia whined. 'This is the girl from Precious Gems who pushed me down the stairs at the theatre.'

Pauline Quaver narrowed her eyes and shook a fat finger like an uncooked pork sausage at Topaz.

'I don't know how you dare show your red face here!' she hissed. 'You're just an amateur who shouldn't be around professionals!'

Topaz was furious. 'She fell!' she said indignantly. 'She wouldn't tie her hair back and her nose was too big.'

'Mum!' squealed Octavia, pretending to look hurt. 'Don't let her speak to you like that!'

60

Mrs Quaver glowered at Topaz. 'My little star has been in plaster for weeks. She's way behind in her dancing lessons, aren't you, baby?'

'I am,' Octavia pouted.

Before Topaz could defend herself, Leo Bluff clapped his hands. 'Stand in line with your forms and we'll call you over, one by one.'

'Excuse me!' Pauline Quaver called out. 'There's no need for my daughter to be in the line-up. I've brought a set of portrait photographs, examples of other ad campaigns she's been in and a full list of her professional engagements.'

Mrs Quaver hauled several photograph albums out of her bag and, thrusting them under Lenny and Leo's noses, began to flip through the pages.

'Octavia's *very* experienced,' she said. 'Just look at the size of her portfolio.'

The men seemed impressed by

Octavia's pictures and huddled together for a whispered conversation.

Octavia gave an annoying little cough and smiled sweetly at Lenny and Leo. 'I'm just so exhausted from coming up those stairs I don't think I could possibly stand.'

'Of course,' said Leo Bluff in a soothing voice. 'Lenny and I will talk to you separately. Just relax until later.'

Mrs Quaver snapped the photograph album shut with a triumphant smile and Octavia smirked.

Topaz was seething. Octavia was even using her broken leg as a way to get special attention.

'Why aren't you on crutches?' she asked her.

Octavia curled her lip and nodded towards Melody Sharp who was still leaning against the doorframe, panting heavily. 'Who needs crutches when I've got her?' she snarled.

*   *   *

Nine girls stood in a line-up whilst Lenny and Leo examined each one as if they were in an identity parade. Ruby was still a bag of nerves and kept her head down and her mouth stuffed with one of her red plaits. She was relieved when Leo whispered in her ear that she wasn't suitable and she gratefully scuttled away from the line-up. One by one, the others were asked to sit on the stool under the large white umbrella, where they pouted and purred whilst Lenny looked through his camera lens.

When it was Sapphire's turn, she left the line-up and, tucking her long legs beneath her, perched prettily on the stool.

Lenny saw her through his camera lens and almost knocked over the tripod with delight.

'I don't believe it!' he shrieked. 'You're Vanessa Stratton's daughter!'

Sapphire blushed and nodded. The other girls looked at Sapphire and glowered. Octavia sat rigidly in her chair, her lips set in a tight snarl. Topaz's stomach lurched. They were all thinking the same thing. They were doomed. The part was Sapphire's. How could they compete with the daughter of a famous film star?

'I'm *such* a fan of your mother's,' Lenny gushed. 'The best close-up in the business.'

A disappointed sigh rang around the room, and the remaining girls in the line-up began to stuff their forms back in their bags and make their way to the door. They knew when they were beaten. Topaz was beginning to wish she hadn't forged the form for Sapphire.

Leo Bluff smiled down at Sapphire and said, 'I'm delighted to meet you and I'm big fan of your mother's, but I'm afraid we can't use you.'

Lenny turned a violent shade of red and almost exploded with fury. 'What!' he spluttered. 'Why?'

'We need real people with real lives,' continued Leo. 'We're aiming for the ordinary girl in the street, not the daughter of a film star.'

Sapphire wanted to grab Leo by the collar, shake him and say, 'I'm trying to be ordinary but no one will let me,' but instead she just gave Leo a watery smile and got up from the stool.

Lenny handed her his business card. 'I'd love to do a photo spread of the Strattons at Christmas for one of the glossies,' he said. 'We'd have to shoot it in July, of course. Will you ask your mother to contact me?'

Sapphire slipped the card into her pocket and walked away from the line-up. She certainly wouldn't be giving her mother the card—however would she explain how she'd come to be at the casting without her permission?

With Sapphire gone, a sigh of relief echoed round the studio as the other girls scrambled back into the line-up, smoothing their hair and practising their smiles.

At last it was Topaz's turn. With Sapphire out of the way and Octavia's huge spot, surely the part was hers? She strode confidently towards the centre of studio, handed Leo her form, smoothed down her hair and went to sit on the stool under the umbrella. But before her bottom had even hit the seat, she heard Pauline Quaver hiss from the sidelines, 'Amateur!'

Topaz scowled at Mrs Quaver, who stuck her nose in the air.

Octavia was draped in her chair as if it was a throne. She stuck her tongue out at Topaz, who glared back.

'Beetroot face!' goaded Pauline Quaver as Octavia giggled and said in a loud whisper, 'Ooh, Mum, you are awful!'

Topaz pulled what she hoped was an insulting face. It was obvious that Pauline and Octavia Quaver were doing their best to wreck her chances of being in the advert, but she wouldn't let them. This was her big chance and they weren't going to spoil it. She looked up at Lenny 'The Lens'.

'Sorry about that,' she said. 'I'm ready for my close-up.'

Lenny looked up from his camera.

'Ready?' he spluttered. The girl obviously hadn't heard the sound of an artist at work. 'Didn't you hear the click of the shutter or the whirr of winding film? We've finished photographing you.'

Topaz was about to leap to her feet and plead for another chance when Leo stepped forward and said, 'You are just what we are looking for! You couldn't *be* more perfect!'

CHAPTER SIX

The after-effects of the Zit Stop! casting affected each of the girls in different ways.

Topaz still couldn't believe that she had got the part in the advert, but Leo Bluff had said she was perfect and that they would be using the photographs Lenny had snapped whilst Topaz wasn't looking. Topaz couldn't remember Lenny even taking any photographs of her, let alone smiling and posing like the other girls had done, but obviously star quality had shone through and she was the chosen one. Zelma Flint had been in touch with Miss Diamond, who had confirmed to Topaz that her face would be used. Topaz thought of Octavia Quaver and her horrid pushy mother and smiled.

I'd love to see their *faces when they find out* my *face is the face of Zit Stop!* she thought to herself.

She couldn't wait to see the advert! She'd told everyone she knew that she was going to be the face of Zit Stop! Her mum, Lola, was proud of her too and had told everyone *she* knew. Strangers would approach Topaz in the street and say, 'Your mum tells me you're doing well at stage school. Congratulations on breaking into advertising!' Topaz had no idea who these people were but when she described them, her mum would say, 'Oh, that's Mrs So and So. I clean for her.'

'But how do they know it's me?' Topaz asked her mum, when yet another strange woman with a plummy voice and expensive highlights had stopped her on the street and congratulated her.

'I keep a picture of you in my purse!'

said Lola, proudly. 'I've probably shown it to them.'

Topaz grimaced. 'Mum!' she said. 'That photo is years old! I was, like, tiny and didn't have any front teeth when it was taken.'

Lola smiled. 'You look beautiful,' she said, as her daughter wondered how much it might cost to get Lenny 'The Lens' to take some proper photographs with airbrushing and nice lighting, now that she had all her teeth.

Sapphire despaired of ever escaping her background and the Stratton name and was seriously considering changing her surname to something more ordinary and less recognizable. Perhaps she'd have to change her first name too. If she'd been called something else she could have lied when Lenny 'The Lens' had asked her whether she was Vanessa Stratton's daughter.

News of Ruby's behaviour at the casting had got back to Adelaide Diamond. It wasn't only Ruby who was becoming worried about how she was going to get over her stage fright. Some of the other staff were voicing their concerns, particularly Anton Graphite who, along with Gloria Gold, had been to see Miss Diamond, demanding she did something.

'Glo and I are at our wits' end, aren't we, Glo?' cried the Artistic Director, throwing up his hands in despair.

Gloria Gold, the Director of Music, nodded. 'Anton's right,' she said through tight lips. 'That's why we're here and we want to know, what *are* you going to do about it?'

Adelaide Diamond looked at her two most senior members of staff, sitting expectantly in front of her. No one ever seemed to come into her office with good news. It was always arguments to be settled or problems to be solved. Being a headmistress was so much harder than being an actress.

'I suppose you're talking about Topaz,' she said wearily.

Neither Anton nor Gloria had supported her decision to offer Topaz a scholarship at Precious Gems, and although Topaz had worked hard to come up to the standard of the other pupils—who already had some dance and musical training—she knew they were just waiting for Topaz to fail, to prove they were right. Perhaps listening to Zelma Flint and letting Topaz go to the casting was a mistake after all.

'Has getting the part in the advert gone to her head *already*?' asked Adelaide.

'Not Topaz,' said Anton, rolling his eyes, and unable to resist adding, 'for a change.'

'It's Ruby,' said Gloria, anxiously wringing her hands. 'Her stage fright is getting worse. Now she won't even perform in class.'

Miss Diamond nodded in agreement. Anton and Gloria's comments came as no surprise. When she'd asked Pearl Wong how the Zit Stop! casting had gone, Pearl had reported that Ruby had been so nervous she hadn't been able to look at the photographer, even for the Polaroid shot. All that Lenny and Leo had seen was a picture of the top of Ruby's head.

'We've tried, Adelaide,' said Gloria earnestly. 'Heaven knows we've tried. I even arranged for her to accompany some of the senior pupils on the piano, in the *Swan Lake* ballet class Anton was taking. Didn't I, Anton?'

Anton pursed his lips and folded his arms across his chest. 'A complete disaster!' he spluttered. 'A simple piece of Tchaikovsky to accompany the scene where the swan dies, and what happens?' He threw his hands in the air again. 'She suddenly stopped playing and bolted out of the class!'

'She didn't even wait until the swan was dead,' sniffed Gloria, shaking her head. '*And* she took the sheet music with her, so I couldn't step in and rescue the situation. Everyone was *very* upset.'

'I'll talk to her,' said Adelaide Diamond, not having the faintest idea was she was going to say.

*   *   *

73

'There has to be some way of helping you, Ruby,' said Miss Diamond. 'I think that next term we must get you to perform in assembly once a week.' She looked at the sobbing, bespectacled redhead in front of her.

'With Topaz?' sniffed Ruby.

Topaz had suggested to Ruby that whenever she wanted to play the piano, she could perform alongside her. Topaz said she hadn't used any props for that first assembly and it had been a spur of the moment decision; but give her time, a proper pair of tap-shoes and a satin-covered top hat and they could perform as a double act.

Miss Diamond shuddered at the thought of Topaz performing for the school every week. The girl would *never* get any work done. She'd spend all day practising her performance.

'*Without* Topaz,' said Miss Diamond firmly.

Ruby looked at the Headmistress with red-rimmed, frightened eyes.

'I don't want to be in adverts like Topaz, so what difference does it make that I was nervous?'

Miss Diamond felt sorry for Ruby. She was a very talented musician, and really should be at a music academy rather than a stage school. But how could you be a professional musician if you couldn't perform in public?

'But it's not just the casting, is it?' said Miss Diamond, gently. 'Miss Gold told me that you didn't wait for the swan to die in *Swan Lake* before you ran out of the room.'

Ruby began to sob more loudly.

'And you *do* want to play the piano, don't you?' asked Miss Diamond.

Ruby looked up and nodded enthusiastically. Music was the only thing she felt she was good at. She was of average ability for schoolwork, terrible at dancing and *really* terrible at sports, but from an early age she'd been able to play the piano and read music, much to the astonishment of her parents, both of whom were tone deaf.

Ruby snorted back snotty tears and fiddled nervously with her handkerchief.

'Everyone says that once I get on the

75

stage my nerves will disappear but they don't, they get worse!'

Miss Diamond handed Ruby a clean tissue. 'You were fine when you appeared on the game show last term. What was so different about that?'

Ruby thought back to the time when she'd appeared on the cookery game show *Proof of the Pudding* with Topaz and Sapphire.

'I wasn't wearing my glasses so I couldn't see the audience, but if I don't wear my glasses when I'm playing, I can't see the music.' Ruby blew her nose and added sadly, 'Perhaps I should leave and go to an ordinary school. Perhaps I'll just become a piano tuner.'

CHAPTER SEVEN

'Hypnosis,' said Topaz when Ruby tearfully recounted the conversation with Miss Diamond to her and Sapphire. 'That's the answer to your stage fright.'

'Do you think it might work?' asked Ruby anxiously. 'Do you know anything about it?'

Topaz nodded enthusiastically. 'I saw a programme once about a man who had a fear of onions and he was cured.'

'Don't be silly,' said Ruby, who couldn't see what onions had to do with her stage fright. 'It's not the same thing at all. *I* could collapse in front of a whole concert hall or give a terrible performance and make a complete fool of myself, but what harm can an onion do?'

'Ah, but that's where you're wrong,' said Topaz excitedly. 'When he was young, he slipped on an onion that had rolled off the conveyer belt at the supermarket checkout, hit his head on a pile of baskets, was off school for weeks and missed being selected for the junior trials of Starbridge United Football Club. That one stray onion was a disastrophe for him.'

'How horrible!' agreed Sapphire. 'I had no idea that onions were so dangerous!'

'It's the skins,' said Topaz knowledgeably. 'They're *very* slippery.'

'Go on,' said Ruby, who was becoming interested.

'He lived his whole life in fear of onions. Before hypnosis he would run past the vegetable aisle in supermarkets, wearing dark glasses with a newspaper over his head in case he spotted an evil onion.'

'But surely that was worse because he couldn't see to avoid them?' said Sapphire.

Topaz ignored her. This was a good story and she was enjoying telling it.

'He knew he had to get help when, one day as he was rushing past a pile of onions, one fell off and rolled in front of him. He was frozen in terror in the vegetable aisle until someone bundled him into a trolley and wheeled him outside.'

'That's like me on stage!' exclaimed Ruby. 'I become frozen with fear and can't move!'

'Exactly,' said Topaz. 'And now, after hypnosis, he can juggle onions, even eat them!'

'What a result!' said Sapphire.

'There was a downside, though,' said Topaz.

Ruby looked crestfallen. For one moment, she'd thought hypnosis might be the answer for her too.

'What?' asked Ruby and Sapphire in

unison.

'His breath smelt horrible from eating all the onions and so he had no friends.'

'But at least he had conquered his fear!' said Ruby. 'And it's not as if I am going to be eating pianos!'

Sapphire yawned and stretched her long legs. 'It doesn't always work,' she said. 'At least it didn't for my mother.'

Topaz looked at Sapphire with surprise. 'Your mother had stage fright?'

It seemed impossible to believe that the glamorous Vanessa had ever been anything but at home in front of an audience.

Sapphire shook her head.

'She was scared of onions?' enquired Ruby.

'No. She tried to hypnotize my father with a diamond bracelet when he locked the drinks cabinet and couldn't remember where he'd left the key.'

'I wonder why it worked on Onion Man but not your father?' said Topaz.

'It didn't work because at first, when he saw the diamonds swinging before his eyes, he'd been furious that M was spending money on yet *more* jewellery and then even more furious when she told him it was a present from her latest leading man.'

Topaz was puzzled. 'Why would your dad be annoyed that your mum had a present from another actor?'

Something about the way Sapphire blushed slightly and mumbled, 'It's complicated,' told Ruby and Topaz not to ask any more questions about the diamond bracelet or Vanessa's leading men.

'We might as well give it a go,' said Topaz. 'Are you up for it, Rubes?'

Ruby nodded. She had nothing to lose and it probably wouldn't work anyway.

*   *   *

The girls looked around for something to use. No one had a watch on a chain or any jewellery because Anton Graphite had banned it.

'All that gold flapping about the face spoils the line!' he would say when he

81

spotted a gold chain.

They tried a scarf with a knot in the end but Ruby said it made her feel dizzy. In the end, they decided on a ballet shoe on the end of a ribbon. But every time Topaz lifted the ballet shoe in front of Ruby, someone came into the locker room.

'This is hopeless!' said Ruby. 'I'm never going to get hypnotized.'

'We've got to stop people getting in,' said Topaz.

'We can't stop people getting to their own lockers!' exclaimed Sapphire. 'That will look *very* odd.'

'I've another idea,' said Topaz. 'Follow me.'

The girls trooped out of the locker room and into the corridor. Topaz stopped outside the toilets.

'Right,' she said to Sapphire. 'You stand there and keep people from coming in.'

'How I am going to do that?' demanded Sapphire. 'You can't stop someone going to the loo!'

Topaz looked exasperated. Sometimes Sapphire had *no*

imagination.

'Tell them someone is puking or something,' she said, pushing Ruby through the door.

Ruby sat on one of the toilet seats whilst Topaz crouched in front of her, swinging the ballet shoe.

'Follow the shoe,' said Topaz in a low voice. 'Follow the shoe.'

'I still feel dizzy!' said Ruby, going cross-eyed behind her glasses.

'Just follow the shoe!' demanded Topaz. 'Think of Onion Man.'

Ruby's eyes followed the ballet shoe.

'Left and right. Left and right. Left and right.'

Topaz's voice became even lower.

'You are the greatest concert pianist in the world. When you see the conductor's baton raised and then lowered you will *immediately* feel more confident and imagine yourself playing confidently in front of hundreds of people. Watch the shoe. Left and right. Left and right.'

Topaz continued telling Ruby what a brilliant pianist she would become until Ruby appeared to be in a trance. Topaz began to become a little worried that the hypnosis was working *too* well. Perhaps it was time to bring her out of it.

'When I count backwards from ten to one you will awake refreshed and convinced you are the greatest concert pianist in the world. Ten, nine, eight . . . you are beginning to wake feeling refreshed.'

Ruby didn't move. Her eyes remained fixed on the swinging ballet shoe. Topaz began to feel uneasy.

'Seven, six, five, four . . .' Ruby still remained glassy-eyed, following the ballet shoe. *Why wasn't Ruby looking normal?* Topaz thought frantically. 'Three! Two!'

'What's going *on*?' shouted a senior pupil as she burst through the door of the toilets before Topaz had the chance to say 'One'.

CHAPTER EIGHT

'Do you think it's worked?' asked Ruby anxiously, rubbing her head as they made their way to a geography lesson. Topaz had been startled when the senior pupil had burst in on them. She'd accidentally whacked Ruby on the forehead with the hard blocked end of the swinging ballet shoe, sending her reeling backwards, hitting the back of her head on the toilet cistern. She still looked a little dazed.

'If Miss Diamond asked you to play in assembly or go to an audition, how would you feel?' asked Sapphire.

Ruby turned pale and little beads of sweat immediately appeared on her forehead.

'Sick,' she groaned. 'But that might just be from the whack on the head.'

'It's not surprising it hasn't worked,' said Topaz, a touch irritated. 'That senior rushing in stopped me counting backwards.' She paused outside the classroom.

'Aren't you coming in?' asked Sapphire.

Topaz shook her head. 'At the last possible minute,' she said, leaning against the doorframe. 'I'll see you in there.'

Topaz hated being cooped up in the classroom. She just didn't see the point of going to stage school if you still had normal lessons. At this very minute, Kylie Slate and her old best friend Janice Stone would be sitting in a classroom at Starbridge High doing *exactly* the same lessons as Topaz. And would they be famous stars? Of course not!

She fished in her bag, pulled out the latest copy of *Snapped!* magazine and looked at the pictures of Sapphire's mother lying in the sun. Topaz's mother would never make the pages of *Snapped!* There wasn't much call for cleaners in celebrity magazines. Topaz thought it strange that Sapphire hadn't seemed the slightest bit interested that her mother was featured.

I'd be putting the article on the school notice-board if it was someone in my family, thought Topaz. Her mum had a very good voice. She'd heard her sing at birthday parties and weddings but these days she only sang in the bath.

I wonder how my life would have turned out if my mother had decided to become a singer rather than a cleaner, she thought to herself.

As Topaz stood reading *Snapped!*, a sarcastic voice asked, 'Are you going to grace us with your presence today, Miss L'Amour?'

Looking over the top of her magazine she saw two huge feet wearing shoes like Cornish pasties, attached to legs swathed in brown corduroy.

87

'Hello, Mr Feldspar,' she said, looking up at the geography teacher. 'Do I have to?'

Do I *have to?* Bob Feldspar wanted to scream at Topaz. *Do I really have to teach geography to a class of pupils who would rather be tap-dancing than learning about precipitation and cloud formation? You're not the only one who would rather stay this side of the door!*

Bob Feldspar was a bitter man. The position of Geography Master at Precious Gems had seemed an ideal opportunity for a man who loved his subject but was also a bit of a leading light in the local amateur dramatics group, the Starbridge Strollers. People still talked in awe about his pirate in *The Pirates of Penzance*, and if his wife hadn't had yet *another* baby, he might have been tempted to throw in the chalk, give up teaching and become a professional actor. Teaching at a stage school seemed the next best thing. But he hadn't thought about the fact that none of the pupils wanted to learn anything that wasn't to do with the theatre, or that the theatrical staff wanted nothing to do with the academic staff. As a geography teacher with a sideline in amateur dramatics, he was despised by both sets of teachers and all of his pupils. He knew everyone called him Fusty Feldspar behind his back. He looked at Topaz L'Amour lounging outside the classroom. She had everything in front of her: the potential for stardom, a career in show business, dreams! *His* dreams of stardom were in tatters. All he had in front of him was a class of bored first-years. No wonder he felt resentful of Topaz.

He held the door open and said bitterly, 'We all have to do things we don't want,' as they both trudged reluctantly through the door.

What a waste of time! Topaz thought as she slung her bag on the floor and slumped into a chair at the back of the class. Would learning about the characteristics of a river channel help get her a part in a leading West End production? How would knowing about changing landscapes give her an edge over Octavia Quaver at an audition? Octavia was probably at a casting right now—becoming known, filling her portfolio with adverts, smiling at casting directors, not sitting surrounded by textbooks.

Topaz flicked open her geography book and began practising her autograph, filling page after page with Topaz L'Am♥ur, occasionally smiling and nodding as she pretended she was handing it back to an adoring fan.

She was suddenly aware of the large, corduroy-clad frame of Bob Feldspar standing by her desk. All her classmates swivelled their heads to look at her.

'I'm pleased to see you have been busy making so many notes, Topaz,' said Mr Feldspar, curling his top lip. 'This is one lesson you obviously find interesting.'

Topaz gave a watery smile and closed her exercise book.

The teacher glared at her with steely eyes. 'As we all know how fond you are of an audience, perhaps you would like to come out to the front of the class and help me with the lesson?'

This was one performance Topaz would have preferred to miss, but the teacher hadn't so much *asked* her to come to the front of the class as *ordered* her. She pushed back her chair and made her way to the front of the room. Nineteen pairs of eyes followed her.

Hanging from the blackboard was a huge map.

'So,' said Bob Feldspar, with a smug smile, handing her a long ruler, 'perhaps you could point out where on the coastline that we are studying you could expect the highest incidence of chalk formation.'

Topaz stared at the map. It showed one huge lump with wavy borders. She turned back to the class and could see Sapphire trying to mouth her the answer, but it didn't help. Even if she'd been able to lip-read she still wouldn't have known where to point on the map.

Bob Feldspar had a triumphant look in his eye. He'd been complaining about Topaz L'Amour's lack of concentration in the class since she'd arrived at Precious Gems. She'd never been the most attentive of pupils but so far this term she'd been particularly bad. Sending Topaz to professional castings was a mistake. Trudi Tuffstone, the science mistress, agreed with him. The one person who didn't was Adelaide Diamond. Why did she always stick up for Topaz?

'Any more problems, Bob, and I'll have a word with her,' the Headmistress had said.

Now he had evidence of Topaz's lack of concentration!

'Come on, Topaz,' he said, letting a twisted grin creep across his face. 'Show us what you have learnt.'

Topaz felt trapped. If she didn't point out something she would be in trouble; but if she did, it would obviously be the wrong place and she'd *still* be in trouble. She'd just have to pick somewhere and point to it convincingly. She knew she could be a good actress and now was a chance to play the part of a pupil who had been listening intently to the lesson, even if she hadn't.

Peering at the map, she saw a name she recognized. Boddington Sands. Her mum had taken her there for a weekend a few years ago. She didn't know much about it, but it was the only name she recognized and it *was* on the coast. She remembered having a ride on a bad-tempered donkey on the beach. It was as good a place as any.

She took a deep breath, and, tapping the seaside town with the ruler, announced confidently, 'The coastline surrounding Boddington Sands has the highest incidence of chalk formation.'

The geography teacher's mouth fell open. He'd been sure he'd had a golden opportunity to humiliate Topaz.

'That's right,' he said in a high-pitched, strangulated voice as the class giggled. He noticed Topaz smiling triumphantly. He wasn't going to let her make a fool of him in front of the others. He'd make her suffer.

'Perhaps you'd like to continue to point at the area whilst I finish discussing the surrounding flora and fauna,' he growled.

Topaz's arm began to ache as she continued to hold the ruler over Boddington Sands. She knew he was just doing it to get back at her, so she stood holding the ruler high above her head and looked round the class.

No one seemed very interested in what the teacher was saying, except Sapphire who was scribbling proper notes in her exercise book. Behind her glasses, Ruby had a strange, glazed expression. Topaz tried to catch her eye but Ruby didn't even seem to be blinking.

Topaz's arm became unbearably heavy and the ruler felt like a lead weight, but there was no way she was going to give Fusty Feldspar the satisfaction of asking if she could put her hand down.

Finally, Mr Feldspar looked at the clock and began to draw the lesson to a close. He turned to Topaz and said, 'You can put your arm down now,

Topaz.'

With a sigh of relief, Topaz let her arm fall, the long ruler hitting the desk as she did so.

Immediately, Ruby pushed back her chair, tossed her red plaits over her shoulder, nodded to the class and began to bang on her desk as if she was playing the piano.

The class stared. Ruby looked possessed.

Up and down the desk her nimble fingers flew, momentarily stopping to flip over the pages of her exercise book as if it were sheet music, her feet pressing imaginary pedals.

'Ruby Ruddle!' shouted Mr Feldspar. 'What's going on?'

On and on Ruby played. One minute she was playing great piano concertos, her face contorted with emotion. The next, she was smiling and winking at the class as she swayed to imaginary jazz.

The class began to roar with laughter. Only Topaz and Sapphire stared at each other in horror. Ruby was still hypnotized! When Topaz had brought the ruler down, Ruby must have thought it was a conductor's baton and she was playing in a concert!

Bob Feldspar clapped his hands to try to get Ruby to stop, but Ruby thought it was applause and stood up to take a bow before announcing, 'For my encore, I shall be playing a selection of songs from well-known musicals!'

There was nothing for it but to try and finish the hypnotism there and then.

'*One!*' screamed Topaz at the top of her voice.

Ruby immediately stopped playing and looked around. Everyone was staring at her.

'What?' she asked, looking puzzled. 'What are you all staring at?'

CHAPTER NINE

'Whose idea was it to hypnotize Ruby?' Miss Diamond asked Topaz and Sapphire as they stood, shamefaced, in front of her desk.

'Mine,' admitted Topaz, shifting nervously from one foot to the other. 'I saw a programme about a man and an onion.'

'And a little bit mine,' added Sapphire. 'I told Topaz about the locked drinks cabinet and my mother's diamond bracelet.'

Topaz couldn't let Sapphire take any of the blame, even if she had been a rotten guard outside the toilets.

'It really wasn't anything to do with

Sapphire,' she said. 'It was *my* idea. I swung the ballet shoe in the toilet cubicle.'

Adelaide Diamond rubbed her eyes. It had been a long day. She had no idea what onions, diamond bracelets and ballet shoes in toilets had to do with hypnotizing Ruby Ruddle, and was too tired to ask.

'How is she?' asked Topaz anxiously. No one had seen Ruby after Miss Diamond had been called to the classroom and led the bewildered first-year away.

'She's fine,' said Miss Diamond. 'I managed to get in contact with the Great Hamboni and luckily, he was able to break the hypnotic trance.'

Topaz remembered the magician from the Starbridge Christmas Show.

'Will there be any lasting effects?' asked Sapphire nervously. If she'd managed to stop that pupil bursting into the toilets before Topaz had finished, none of this might have happened.

'The Great Hamboni says she still looks a little confused when she sees rulers, but at least she isn't playing Beethoven on her desk,' said Miss Diamond, still wondering whether to telephone Ruby's parents about the incident. She thought about Ruby's highly-strung mother and decided against it.

'Topaz, you sit down and stay here. Sapphire,' she said, 'I suggest you go home and keep away from anyone who approaches you with an onion or a ballet shoe.' She nodded towards the door.

'Thank you, Miss Diamond,' said Sapphire, scrambling to pick up her bag. 'I'm *really* sorry.'

Topaz sat on the lumpy sofa and waited for both the sofa springs and Miss Diamond to erupt with anger the moment Sapphire left the room, but instead, the sofa just sagged. Miss Diamond slumped back in her chair and ran her fingers through her coarse grey hair. She was normally so composed, so calm, so in control, but this afternoon she looked tired, slightly defeated and very sad.

'Topaz, I'm *very* disappointed in you,' she said with a sigh.

Topaz's stomach lurched and to her surprise, she felt hot tears spring in her eyes. She could cope with Miss D being angry with her, but not disappointed.

'There are people here who didn't want you to come to Precious Gems,' said Miss Diamond, thinking of Anton Graphite and Gloria Gold. 'People who thought you wouldn't fit in here.'

Topaz forgot her tears for a moment and began plotting her revenge against whoever these people were.

Miss Diamond continued. 'I stuck my neck out and offered you a place, but you've let me down.'

'But I've worked hard at dance and singing and music and theatre!' protested Topaz. 'You said so last term when you offered me a part in the Christmas show!'

Miss Diamond nodded. 'I agree, Topaz. I agree. But sometimes it takes more luck than talent to succeed in show business. That's why *this* stage school isn't just about being a performer. It's about education, living within rules, skills you'll need for everyday life. If you leave here only able to count on your fingers, then even if you have a career in show business, I will have failed you!'

Topaz sniffed and wiped her eyes on her blazer. Miss Diamond was worrying about nothing. 'But I *will* be in show business, Miss Diamond!' she said, her voice trembling. 'It won't matter that I can only count on my fingers if my name's in lights!'

Miss Diamond looked at Topaz and remembered the auditions. Off stage, everything about Topaz was just average, but on it, she shone from within. She remembered her leaving the stage and how it had somehow seemed smaller and duller without her. But as she knew from experience, a life in show business was hard, and Topaz had a long way to go before she could be sure of making a career in the limelight.

'I'm sorry, Topaz,' Adelaide said calmly, 'but for the rest of the school year there can be no more adverts, no more castings, no more game shows. The rest of the year *must* be spent concentrating on schoolwork.'

'But!' exclaimed Topaz, wide-eyed with despair.

'But nothing,' said Miss Diamond firmly. 'This is your *last chance*, Topaz. Let me down again and your scholarship will be withdrawn. After that, if you want to stay at Precious Gems, your mother will have to pay your school fees.'

Topaz looked broken-hearted. She pulled herself off the sofa and began to make her way to the door. Even the sofa springs didn't seem to have the heart to spring back in the vicious way they usually did. Topaz turned back for a moment, looked at Miss Diamond with a tear-stained face, and left, quietly shutting the door behind her.

Adelaide Diamond buried her head in her hands as a tear rolled down her wrinkled cheek. It took every ounce of self-control for her not to run after Topaz shouting, 'I'm just doing this for your own good! I'd never really let you go.'

*   *   *

Topaz slowly walked down the steps of the school. It was getting dark and the cars swishing down Stellar Terrace already had their lights on. Perhaps she would walk around the streets for a bit. The girls from Starbridge High would probably be waiting at the bus stop after hanging round the shops, and she just couldn't face bumping into them. Life had been so much easier before she'd gone to stage school. At Starbridge Middle, no one seemed to notice if you handed homework in late, or even not at all. She'd had Janice as a best friend, and they'd spent hours in each other's bedrooms, listening to music, reading magazines, swapping gossip—or wandering round Starbridge, trying on clothes they couldn't afford, hanging round the chip shop, playing with the make-up samples in Wellington's the Chemist until the assistants told them to leave. Sapphire and Ruby were friends, but it wasn't the same. She'd never been invited to Sapphire's house in the posh suburb of Starbridge Hill, although she'd seen pictures of it in *Celebrity Pools & Patios* magazine. Ruby went home to Sutton Perry at weekends—not that Topaz even knew where Sutton Perry was. Ruby said it was *miles* away. The after-school dance and music lessons Topaz had to take to catch up with the others meant there was hardly any time to spend together, and most of the other pupils in her class hung round with the friends they'd made in after-school drama clubs or dancing classes before they'd come to Precious Gems.

Sometimes, Topaz thought sadly to herself, *I don't think I fit in anywhere or with anybody*.

As she walked up Galaxy Street, she noticed the lights of Happy Al's Café blazing and the sign on the door still turned to 'Open'. Perhaps a hot chocolate would make her feel better.

She pushed open the door, walked in and looked around for somewhere to sit. Al was mopping the floor, the

chairs standing on the red-checked tables along with the ketchup bottles and salt and pepper pots. Without looking up he barked, 'We're closed.'

He glanced up, and to his surprise, saw Topaz silently making her way towards the door, head down, shoulders drooping. Normally, he would have put money on her giving some smart retort. She didn't look like the feisty Topaz he'd seen before.

'Wait!' called Al, leaning on his mop. 'I can't do you a cheese toastie or an all-day breakfast, but I can do you a hot drink.'

Topaz gave him a grateful smile and, removing one of the chairs from a nearby table, sat down. 'Thanks,' she said. 'A hot chocolate, please.'

Al disappeared behind the counter, and, after a series of strange noises and

105

a puff of steam, brought over a cup of frothy hot chocolate. Topaz began to rummage in her purse for money, but Al surprised himself by saying, 'On the house.' Since Topaz and Ruby had won *Proof of the Pudding* with his chocolate mousse recipe, business had been brisk, and Al was secretly grateful to Topaz for mentioning the café on the show.

'Thanks!' said Topaz, blowing on the top of the chocolate.

As Al continued to mop the floor, he couldn't help but notice Topaz staring forlornly into her steaming mug. He went over to the table, took down another chair and sat down.

'Trouble at home?' he asked.

Topaz shook her head.

'Boy trouble?'

'No!' said Topaz, blushing slightly.

'School?'

Topaz's shoulders drooped even further and she nodded.

'If I don't do better at school, Miss D will take away my scholarship and I'll have to leave Precious Gems. Mum can't afford the fees.'

'I thought all that singing and dancing and stuff was everything you dreamt of?' said Al. 'You given up already?'

Topaz shook her head. 'The stage stuff isn't the problem. It's hard work, but I know *why* I'm working hard. I want my name in lights. I want my name in the theatre programme. I don't want to just be *a* face in the crowd. I want to be *the* face in the crowd. The star! Miss Diamond says I have talent but . . .'

'But what?' asked Al.

'I don't like schoolwork. I mean, *proper* schoolwork. Maths and science and stuff. Those subjects are no use to me! Miss D says I have to get better grades in class or I'm on my own. She says'—Topaz paused as if the words were too painful to say—'sometimes it takes more luck than talent to succeed.'

Al sat back in his chair and put his hands behind his head. 'She's right, you know,' he said. 'Look at me!'

Topaz looked puzzled.

Al growled, 'Once I was a star. A *big* star. Being Inspector Barry 'Nosey'

Parker opened doors. I had a prime-time TV series, my own table at the Truffle Pig, free entry to the Super Nova Nightclub, pretty girlfriends, my name in lights . . .'

'You had your name in lights?' gasped Topaz. Everyone knew Al had starred in *Murder Mile* before he opened Happy Al's, but she'd never heard him talk about it before.

'Well, not exactly in lights,' admitted Al, 'but in big print in *The Starbridge Gazette*. I *was* somebody. No wonder they called me Happy Al. I couldn't believe my luck. I was a TV star!'

'So how did you end up frying greasy chips all day?' asked Topaz.

Al looked stung. 'The fickle finger of fame and fortune pointed at me,' he said angrily. 'One minute you're hot, the next you're not!' He kicked the table leg so hard, Topaz's hot chocolate slopped over the top of her mug.

'That won't happen to me,' said Topaz confidently. 'I won't let it!'

Al scowled. 'Oh no?' he said. 'So how are you going to stop a new TV boss coming in and changing everything just for the sake of it? How are you going to compete when suddenly *International Speed Tiddlywinks* gets better ratings than you? What are you going to do when your face no longer fits?' He almost spat the words out.

Topaz looked surprised. She'd only come in for a hot chocolate. Not a lesson in show business failure.

'I'd get out at the top and tell my agent to get me a new part!' she said, thinking of Zelma Flint's card in her purse.

Al grabbed Topaz's mug of hot chocolate even though she hadn't finished it.

'We're closing!' he said gruffly, turning the sign on the door to 'Closed'. It pained him to admit it, but young Topaz was right. He *should* have got out at the top, but like so many others, he'd listened to his agent Zelma Flint, rather than his own intuition.

109

*　　　*　　　*

Topaz stood in the bus shelter as yet another packed bus arrived, only for the driver to swiftly pull away when he realized no one was getting off. She'd been much longer in town than she'd intended, and now the buses were full of workers leaving Starbridge to go home for the evening. Topaz's feet began to feel cold, so she hopped about on the spot.

'Oooh, if it isn't Little Miss Wannabe Famous,' sneered a horribly familiar voice. 'Shall *we* be your audience? Come on, dance again!'

Kylie Slate appeared from round the back of the bus shelter, followed by a group of girls, most of whom Topaz recognized.

'Go on, dance!' snarled Kylie.

Topaz ignored them, but they crowded around her. Kylie jabbed her finger towards Topaz. 'Didn't you hear me, Little Miss Wannabe Famous? I said DANCE!'

'Leave her alone!' a voice shouted

110

from the back of the crowd. The Slate
gang turned and stared at Janice Stone.

'You want to dance too, Jan?'
snapped Kylie. 'You could do a nice
little double act.'

Janice remained silent and bit her
lip, but for a moment she looked at
Topaz and a smile danced across her
eyes.

We were such *good friends*, thought
Topaz angrily. *How did we let Precious
Gems and Kylie Slate come between us*?

'You are such a jealous saddo, Slate!'
snapped Topaz, holding her school bag
in front of her for protection. 'You
can't bear it that I'm going to be
famous! I'm already in an advert!'

Some of the other girls looked
impressed. Mutterings rang round the
crowd. An advert! Perhaps Topaz was
going to be famous after all. It might
be worth keeping in with her. She
might be a celebrity.

Kylie Slate looked surprised and
then angry.

She took a step forward and stood
nose to nose with Topaz.

'No one calls me a saddo!' she

hissed.

'Leave her alone, Ky!' shouted Janice.

Kylie spun round and glared at Janice. 'Are you sticking up for Miss Stuck-up?' she almost spat the words at Janice. 'Because if you are, I'm warning you . . .'

Janice hung her head and muttered, 'Let's at least see what the advert looks like.'

Kylie stepped back and addressed her gang. 'She could be lying,' she sneered. 'We don't even know what this advert's for!'

'We do now!' someone piped up.

For there, on the side of the bus which had just pulled up, lit by the fluorescent street lights, was a huge picture of a scowling, red-faced Topaz, covered in spots, next to a clear-skinned, smiling Octavia Quaver out of whose mouth came a speech bubble saying, 'Don't Pop It—Stop It!'

CHAPTER TEN

As the term drew to a close, it seemed no one at Precious Gems was happy.

Topaz sat miserably in class, trying to concentrate as Miss Diamond had told her to, but found it very difficult to get her head round fractions and equations when her head, complete with digitally added spots, kept pulling up on a bus outside the classroom window. Octavia's grinning face seemed to taunt her. *She* wouldn't be sitting in lessons. *She'd* be out and about with her pushy mother, going to auditions, getting parts, tasting fame.

Adelaide Diamond was furious that Zelma Flint had clearly misled her over the extent of the Zit Stop! campaign. A small local print campaign in a few magazines, Zelma had said. Now Topaz was appearing on the side of every bus around Starbridge. Not only that, but Adelaide had learnt that Topaz had only received a tiny fee, whereas Zelma had taken a huge commission. She'd left a number of messages on Zelma's answering machine, making it quite clear that she would *never* be Topaz's agent whilst she was still at Precious Gems. But Zelma didn't return her calls.

Ruby was gloomy; she had decided she would never get over her stage fright and had started having nightmares about spending the rest of her life teaching scales to badly-behaved small children with sticky fingers who would rather be playing computer games than the piano.

Sapphire didn't know why she was miserable. She never expected her mother to come home for the Easter holidays, but found she was upset when it was confirmed that she wouldn't.

But *nobody* was as unhappy as Pearl

Wong the night before the shoot of the new Speedy Snax commercial.

* * *

'How dare you look in my bag?' Pearl snapped at her father. 'How can I ever trust you again?'

'Trust! You talk about trust when you were hiding this?' Mr Wong waved the contract for the next Speedy Snax commercial in the air. 'Noodle Burgers! Sweet 'N' Sour Burgers! Crispy Duck Dippers! Speedy Snax will kill our business! I forbid you to be part of their evil plans!'

Pearl stood sullenly in the family takeaway business whilst her father paced the floor, his face crimson with fury.

Striding to the door of the Wok and Spring Roll, he turned the sign to 'Closed'. Mr Wong *never* turned the sign to 'Closed'. At any time of the day or night, someone might just fancy a portion of egg fried rice and a beef chow mein, and Mr Wong was always there, wok in hand, at the ready.

'What are you doing?' asked Pearl. 'Why are you closing?'

Mr Wong's black eyes blazed. 'Because if you do this advert, we may as well stay closed for ever!'

'If I don't do it, someone else will!' shouted Pearl. 'Someone else will be "Girl Eating Burger".'

Mr Wong banged the counter with his fist. 'Let them!' he cried. 'Let them. But I'll tell you this. Being involved with Speedy Snax is wrong for a Wong!'

The television chattered away in the corner, and the pump on the fish tank burbled, as father and daughter stared at each other in stony silence.

Pearl stood her ground. Her father was usually a kind, mild-mannered man and she knew his temper was only raised because he was worried about the business.

'I'm going to do it whether you like it or not!' she stormed, shattering the silence. 'I'm going to the filming

116

tomorrow and *nothing* you can do will stop me!'

She ran out of the shop, through the kitchen, up the back stairs into her bedroom, and, slamming the door behind her, threw herself on to her bed.

Hot tears rolled down her face. For weeks she'd been telling everyone that she was going to be starring in the new Speedy Snax television commercial. No longer would she just be 'Girl Eating Burger', she would be *the* 'Girl Eating Burger'. If only it wasn't a Sweet 'N' Sour Noodle Burger! Despite telling her father that Speedy Snax wasn't any threat to his business, she knew in her heart of hearts she didn't really believe it—or why had she boasted to everyone about the commercial *except* her father?

*   *   *

'But you have to go!' said Topaz when Pearl told her why she was sitting on the wall outside the school, angrily kicking her heels against the brickwork.

'You *are* "Girl Eating Burger".'

Pearl gave the wall another angry kick. 'I know! Just try telling *him* that.' She nodded towards the Wok and Spring Roll on the corner of Stellar Terrace and Galaxy Street. The curtains in an upstairs window twitched and Topaz could just make out the tiny figure of Mr Wong, peering out from behind the nets.

'He's watching you?' asked Topaz, as Mr Wong darted back behind the curtain.

Pearl nodded. 'He said he was going to make sure I went through the school door in the morning and that he'd watch until I came out in the afternoon.'

'Bummer!' said Topaz, who had secretly envied Pearl living so close to the school, and being able to roll out of bed five minutes before assembly. It hadn't occurred to her that this also meant your parents could spy on you.

'What would happen if you just went?' asked Topaz. 'Just walked away from the school, got on the bus and went to the filming.'

Pearl thought of her father's face filled with disappointment, unhappiness and fear. He'd brought her up on his own since her mum had died after an unfortunate accident with a box of fortune cookies. He was *so* proud of her and despite their argument, she loved him. Going to the shoot without his blessing wasn't an option.

'What's up?' asked Sapphire, appearing from round the corner. She felt that it was embarrassing enough that she lived in stuck-up Starbridge Hill, without letting on that a chauffeur brought her to school, so she made him drop her off in the next street.

'Pearl's dad won't let her be in the next Speedy Snax commercial,' said Topaz. 'It's for Sweet 'N' Sour Noodle Burgers.'

'Bad luck,' said Sapphire. 'When were you due to shoot?'

Pearl put her head in her hands. 'Today,' she wailed. 'At Starbridge Sound and Vision Studios.'

Sapphire raised her eyebrows. 'You'll be popular then!' she said. 'They'll have problems finding someone at the last minute. Directors might even blacklist you for letting them down. My dad says it's better to be a bad actress than an unreliable one.'

Pearl rolled her eyes in despair. 'I'm never going to work in this town again,' she wailed. 'What *am* I going to do?'

Topaz was thinking fast. One girl's disastrophe could be another girl's golden opportunity.

'I've done commercials before!' she said, as a bus drove past with her face on the side. 'I could go in your place. I could be the girl eating a Noodle Burger.'

Pearl looked at the junior pupil as if she were mad. 'Are you bonkers? That was *print*. This is *television*! You can't just wander in off the street and land a part like that. This is the big time, Topaz, and you're an unknown!'

Topaz felt stung. 'I was only trying to help!' she said. Even if she didn't get the part she would have loved the chance to look round the studios. They often had large shiny black cars parked outside, their drivers lolling about on the bonnets wearing black suits and sunglasses, even on a rainy day, while they waited to whisk stars away at the end of filming.

'I'm sorry,' said Pearl. 'But anyway, I thought Miss Diamond said no more commercials until next year?'

Ruby ran down the steps of the school. 'There you are!' she said. 'I've been waiting in the locker room for you. What's going on?'

'Pearl's supposed to be filming a Speedy Snax TV advert today but her dad won't let her and now she's never going to work again unless she can think of something,' said Topaz, who felt she'd summed up the situation perfectly, though she was still miffed that Pearl had called her bonkers.

Ruby shrugged her shoulders. 'Just play the too-ill-to-star card,' she said. 'I've used that excuse loads of times when I've wanted to get out of performing.'

'That's a great idea!' said Pearl, jumping off the wall. 'What's wrong with me?'

Ruby was well practised in the art of excuses not to perform at the last

minute. 'It has to be something serious enough to keep you away from everyone, but not so serious that they start sending you fruit and flowers,' she said. 'It has to come on suddenly, so that no one can blame you for letting them down at the last minute.'

'I know!' shrieked Topaz, jumping up and down. 'I could go to the shoot and say that you fell ill on the bus and I was a passenger and I've been sent to tell them!'

Pearl didn't look convinced. 'What's wrong with me?' she asked.

'It'll have to be quite serious,' replied Sapphire, 'otherwise Dr Showbiz would get you through it, for the filming, at least.'

Topaz gave Sapphire a puzzled look. 'Dr Showbiz?' she asked.

Sapphire casually flicked her long blonde hair over her shoulder. 'You know, the show must go on, even if your leg is falling off!'

'But what's wrong with me?' said Pearl again. 'I need to know what's wrong with me.'

'Don't worry,' said Topaz. 'I'll think of something.'

Black clouds began to gather in the skies and a bell sounded for the first lesson.

'If anyone asks where I am,' yelled Topaz as she headed towards the bus stop, 'tell them I'm not coming in today. Tell them I fell ill on the bus!'

CHAPTER ELEVEN

Topaz stood, dripping wet, in the reception area of Starbridge Sound & Vision Studios. She'd been unable to get on the first bus into Starbridge because when it finally arrived, not only did it have the Zit Stop! poster down one side, it was packed with girls from Starbridge High, including Kylie Slate who had leant out of the window when the bus stopped and drawn glasses and a moustache on Topaz's face. It was bad enough getting on a bus with your face plastered down the side without having to get on a bus with the Slate gang as well. Then the heavens had opened and every bus swept past the stop full of passengers, sending a spray of muddy water up Topaz's skirt.

Eventually, she began to trudge towards downtown Starbridge. At the time, it had seemed like a good idea to go to the shoot, but now she was beginning to worry about what Miss Diamond would say. Suppose she had seen her at the bottom of the steps? Why hadn't she thought to tell the others to tell Miss Diamond that she'd been taken ill on the steps rather than on the bus? Would Sapphire say, 'Oh, Miss Diamond! Topaz suddenly went deathly white and collapsed against the wall and luckily a passing ambulance took her to hospital?' or would she be as laidback as usual and just say, 'She's ill,' causing Miss Diamond to be suspicious? Topaz told herself not to worry. She was only popping into the studios to say that Pearl was ill and then she'd go back to school. What harm could a little white lie possibly do?

*　　　*　　　*

'Sign in,' said a sulky-looking girl on the reception desk who was busy filing her nails.

'I'm just here with a message,' said Topaz.

The girl raised her eyes, but not her head. 'You've still gotta sign in,' she drawled.

Topaz leant over to sign her name and dripped water all over the desk. The sulky girl wiped the desk with her sleeve, sighed and continued to file her nails.

'Write the name of the person or organization you are visiting, together with the time of your arrival,' she said, as if on autopilot.

Topaz was poised mid-signature when a very tall man with a long ponytail burst into the reception area, followed by a nervous-looking woman with a clipboard. The man seemed very flustered. As he leant over the reception desk, Topaz noticed tiny beads of sweat breaking out on his forehead.

'Has no one asked for me?' he

barked at the sulky girl.

The girl stopped filing her nails in mid-file, looked him straight in the eyes and said, 'Nah.'

The man turned to the girl with the clipboard. 'The ad is due to air in days,' he shrieked. 'We could lose the account if it doesn't. It'll be the end of the big time, Natasha! We'll be stuck doing insurance adverts for cable TV!'

Natasha the Clipboard patted his arm and said in a soothing voice, 'Julian, don't upset yourself. It won't come to that. She'll be here. Remember, she's perfect for the campaign.'

Topaz tried again to sign her name.

'Put the name of the person or organization you are visiting, together with the time of your arrival,' Sulky Girl repeated.

Topaz was furious. The least the girl could do was appear interested in what she was doing, even if she wasn't.

Topaz leant over and dripped more water on the desk. The girl looked up. Topaz looked straight back at her.

'*That's* what I have been trying to tell

you,' said Topaz politely but firmly. 'I'm not here to see anyone. I'm here to give the Speedy Snax people a message. It's about Pearl Wong.'

It was as if someone had suddenly turned the sound off. The room became deathly quiet. Julian stopped pacing up and down. Natasha the Clipboard stopped breathing. Sulky Girl stopped filing her nails. Topaz stood still.

Julian walked over to the reception desk with slow deliberate steps as if he had chewing gum stuck to the bottom of his shoes. With wild eyes, he looked down at Topaz who was standing in a puddle of water, her hair plastered to her head and her maroon blazer so sodden it was almost black.

'What—about—Pearl—Wong?' he hissed menacingly.

Topaz remembered what Sapphire had said. To let a director down at the last minute was the worst possible thing an actor could do. Julian was furious. Thank goodness they'd thought about pretending Pearl was ill.

'Pearl isn't coming,' said Topaz. 'She fell ill on the bus on the way here.'

Julian clutched his chest and staggered backwards as if he had been punched. 'Natasha!' he called out. 'Natasha! She's not coming! We're doomed!'

Then, like a man possessed, his head whipped round and he stared at Topaz with blazing eyes.

'If I lose this account I'll make sure that girl *never* works in this town again!' he thundered. 'No one lets Julian Burbank down and gets away with it! What exactly is wrong with Miss Wong?'

Topaz remembered with horror that she'd been supposed to have thought of something on the journey to the studios, but what with the rain and no bus and the Slate gang and worrying about Miss Diamond finding out, she hadn't given it any thought.

Julian Burbank lowered his voice to a growl. 'I'm waiting . . .'

'Bigus fibosis,' lied Topaz. 'Yes, they think it is bigus fibosis.'

Julian raised an eyebrow. 'I've never heard of bigus fibosis,' he said, his eyes glittering with suspicion. 'Have you, Natasha?'

Natasha still looked like a rabbit caught in car headlights but managed a stiff shake of her head.

'It's not as rare as you might think,' said Topaz. 'It comes on *very* suddenly.'

Topaz should have stopped there but she couldn't. She had an audience. She was the centre of attention. Now was the time to give a performance worthy of a Golden Nugget. She gave a huge sigh, lowered her eyes and ran her hand across her wet forehead.

'Poor Pearl,' she said, looking up through damp eyelashes. 'Poor, poor Pearl. One minute she was sitting on the bus, really looking forward to being the Speedy Snax girl again; the next, she was covered in a rash and had slipped under the seat in front, barely breathing. Poor Pearl. Poor, poor Pearl. She's *very* ill.'

Julian's eyes stopped blazing and he

looked concerned.

Topaz wrung her hands and shook her head.

'The last thing she said before she slipped under the seat was, "Tell the Speedy Snax people. Please tell them I'm sorry." '

Natasha the Clipboard burst into tears and even Sulky Girl behind reception wiped her eyes on her sleeve. Topaz felt pleased with her performance, but tried not to smile.

'The poor honey,' murmured Julian. 'Thank you *so* much for coming to tell us. It was very good of you. Is she in hospital? Should we send a complimentary basket of Speedy Snax burgers and fries to her ward?'

'She's not *that* ill!' said Topaz, a little too quickly. The last thing she wanted was Julian contacting Starbridge General and finding out Pearl wasn't really ill. 'What I mean is, she's not in hospital.'

Julian's eyes narrowed in a way that made Topaz nervous. 'But if she's ill enough to miss the shoot, shouldn't she be?' he said.

Topaz realized she'd have to think fast. She buried her face in her hands and wailed, 'The reason she's not in  hospital is that she's still on the bus. Bigus fibosis is *very* contagious and she's in quarantine, on the bus!'

Julian suddenly caught sight of the clock on the wall. He felt very sorry for Pearl Wong. Bigus fibosis sounded horrible. But he was more sorry for himself and the fact that his shoot was already running late because his leading Burger Girl was under the seat of a bus with a contagious rash. The studio was booked for the day and the budget wouldn't allow for another casting session *and* another day in the studio. What *were* they going to do?

Topaz stood in the reception, watching Julian pace up and down, muttering to himself. If *only* she could say, 'Mr Burbank, I could be your burger girl!' Julian would rush over, hug her and say, *'You're* the girl we've *always* been looking for. Pearl Wong has nothing on you. Here is a contract for the Lead Burger. Go and make the advert your own!' The shoot would be saved and she would be a star.

But every time she tried to imagine Julian rushing over to congratulate her, an image of Miss Diamond bursting into the room and rugby tackling Julian, tearing the contract out of his hands, came into her head. No, there was *no way* she could even think about becoming involved in the advert. Miss Diamond would pull her scholarship and she'd have to leave Precious Gems. Even if Rhapsody's gave her a scholarship she'd have to go to classes with the evil Octavia Quaver and her gruesome drippy sidekick, Melody Sharp. Or she'd end up back at Starbridge High where Kylie Slate would make her life a misery and Janice Stone probably still wouldn't talk to her. Topaz picked up her bag and turned towards the door.

'We'll have to find someone today,' Julian was saying to Natasha. 'Call

Zelma Flint and see if she has anyone suitable who can get down here immediately.'

Even though Topaz's brain was shouting, 'Walk away! Walk away!' suddenly she heard a voice exactly like her own saying, 'I'm already on Zelma Flint's books. She's my agent.'

CHAPTER TWELVE

Zelma Flint had been surprised but delighted to receive a phone call from Julian Burbank's assistant, Natasha, asking her to confirm whether Topaz L'Amour was indeed on her books.

That sly old bird Adelaide Diamond has obviously seen the error of her ways and agreed to let me represent Topaz, Zelma thought to herself.

There was no need to bother about paperwork, she'd told Natasha. Topaz was at Precious Gems Stage School, she'd already been in an advert and she was representing her. They could cross the 't's and dot the 'i's later.

Topaz waited in the reception area,

feeling sick with excitement and nerves. It was too late to turn back now. But what about Pearl? Pearl had been good to her when she was new at Precious Gems and now she'd stolen Pearl's part.

Topaz could hear the sound of rapidly approaching footsteps and tried to put the thought of Pearl Wong out of her mind. This was *her* moment. Any minute now she would be whisked off to make-up before being filmed looking lovingly at a Noodle Burger. She tried to flatten her hair but it had got so wet, it was drying at all sorts of odd angles. Her face felt a bit flushed too. It didn't matter, hair and make-up would smooth it down and sort her out.

Natasha the Clipboard appeared. 'We're ready for you, Topaz,' she said.

Topaz gulped. 'Can I just pop to the loo first?' she asked. She didn't know how long filming an advert took and it would be awful to have to leave halfway through.

Natasha nodded and pointed towards a door. Topaz slipped inside to see a familiar but unwelcome face

136

preening herself in the mirror. It was Octavia Quaver.

For a fleeting moment Octavia looked shocked to see Topaz, but then she regained her usual sour expression.

'*I'm* here to record the voice-over for the new Speedy Snax Oriental range,' she sneered, continuing to pat her blonde curls and examine her face. 'What are *you* doing here?'

'Duh!' said Topaz, teasingly. 'I'm in a toilet. What do you think I'm doing?'

She giggled at her joke and grinned. There was nothing that Octavia could say that would spoil this moment. She, Topaz L'Amour, was going to launch Speedy Snax's Oriental range and there was absolutely *nothing* Octavia Quaver could do about it. Octavia might be the voice of Speedy Snax, but who would ever know that?

'I mean, what you are doing at the studios, stupid?' snapped Octavia.

Topaz smiled at Octavia in the mirror and purred, 'I'm the face of the new Noodle Burger.'

Octavia's face looked a picture. Her blonde curls quivered and her mouth tightened into a tiny, tight line. She spun round, faced Topaz and threw a paper towel towards her. 'Oh, no you're not!' she spat.

'Oh, yes I am!' said Topaz.

'Oh, no you're not,' growled another voice. 'And I'll tell you why!'

Erupting from the behind a toilet door like a volcano was Pauline Quaver, Octavia's mother.

Natasha popped her head round the door.

'Everything all right, ladies?' she asked nervously. 'We're running *very* late and Julian's getting *very* stressed.'

'Get Julian!' demanded Mrs Quaver. 'There's something he needs to know about this girl.'

*   *   *

'Is this true?' Julian asked Topaz. He'd had casting meetings in top hotels, grubby offices, and once even in a cowshed in the middle of a field, but never in a ladies' toilet.

Topaz fought back tears and nodded. 'I don't see what difference it makes!' she pleaded.

Pauline Quaver wagged a podgy finger at Julian.

'Don't see what difference it makes! Can't you see what an amateur she is? How can a girl who is the "before" face of Zit Stop! be the face of a Noodle Burger?' Pauline rattled her jewellery impatiently. 'She's got a face like a boiled beetroot and it's riding round Starbridge on the side of a bus!'

'But *she's* in the advert too!' said Topaz, pointing to a hatchet-faced Octavia. 'She's also a face of Zit Stop!'

'Mum! Don't let her speak to me like that,' whined Octavia, pretending to looked hurt.

Pauline Quaver loomed over Topaz and exploded with fury. 'But *she's* the one using the product! *She's* the one everyone wants to be! *She's* the face of success!'

Natasha the Clipboard hovered nervously in the doorway. Julian leant against a basin, his shoulders drooping. When Leo Bluff had called him to discuss what Sir Basil Speedy, owner of Speedy Snax, wanted in his new advertising campaign, Julian had suggested costume characters or some nice animation. Animated characters couldn't forget their lines, throw a tantrum and storm off the set. Animated characters did what you wanted them to, when you wanted them to. If they didn't you just pressed the 'delete' button on the computer.

'Sir Basil never spends enough money,' he'd complained to Leo. 'It's a tight budget and a tight schedule. We can't afford for anything to go wrong. You know how *difficult* actors can be.'

But Leo was adamant. Sir Basil Speedy wanted real people. But it wasn't Leo or Sir Basil who was perched on a basin in the ladies' toilet with two young actresses and a battle-axe of a mother. How he longed to press the 'delete' button!

'You!' Julian pointed at Topaz. 'After what I've heard I can't risk you as the face of Speedy Snax. You'll do the voice-over.' He nodded towards Octavia. 'You can be the Noodle Burger Girl.'

'Yes!' Mrs Quaver punched the air in

 victory and Octavia grinned like a Cheshire cat.

'Off you go!' Pauline Quaver said to Topaz. 'Crawl off and do your little part.'

*　　　*　　　*

Topaz trudged down the corridor after Natasha, thinking of all the things she should have said to Octavia and her mother. She'd been *that* close to being the Noodle Burger girl and Octavia had whipped the part from under her nose. Again!

'Can you wait in there?' said Natasha, nodding towards an open door. 'I won't be long.'

The room Natasha had shown her was small, brightly lit and stank of stale tobacco. Every surface was covered with old plastic coffee cups and ashtrays overflowing with stale cigarette ends. Piles of old newspapers and magazines were stacked up on the

141

cushions of stained and threadbare chairs dotted around the room. In one corner was a trolley piled high with plates of cold burgers, fries and dippers.

Topaz looked at her watch. No one had said anything about lunch and she was getting hungry. She picked up one of the dippers and smelt it.

Must be one of the new Crispy Duck Dippers, she thought as she nibbled the edge. Even though it was chewy, cold and greasy, it didn't taste too bad. *They won't miss a few dippers*, she thought as she popped another couple in her mouth.

Natasha the Clipboard put her head round the door just as Topaz was wiping her greasy mouth on the sleeve of her blazer. Natasha was just about to say something when she caught sight of the trolley full of food and her jaw dropped.

'You haven't touched any of that, have you?' she said in a low voice. '*Please* tell me you haven't touched any.'

Topaz shook her head and kept her

mouth shut. She was sure that bits of Duck Dipper were stuck between her teeth.

'Oh thank goodness!' gasped Natasha as they began to walk down the corridor. 'All that stuff should have been thrown out days ago when we finished photographing it. It's only fit for the bin. It's been sitting around under hot studio lights for days and is probably *teeming* with bugs. The Health and Safety people could sue us!'

They stopped outside a door and Natasha told Topaz to go in.

'Julian will be along in a minute,' she said. 'Tone will look after you.' She gave a shy smile and blushed. 'He's *very* good. He used to be the sound man for the Thrash Metal Monster Maniacs.'

In the sound studio, a man with long hair and a pierced lip sat reading a magazine, his feet resting on a desk studded with lights, buttons, levers, dials and meters. Huge tattooed arms burst from the sleeves of his black skull-and-crossbones T-shirt. He didn't look up when Topaz entered the room.

'Excuse me,' she said, 'are you Tone?'

'Who wants to know?' he replied, continuing to read his magazine.

'I'm here to record the Speedy Snax voice-over,' she said. 'I'm Topaz L'Amour.'

Tone sniffed, slowly swung his legs off the desk, flicked a few levers, pressed a couple of buttons and handed Topaz a huge pair of headphones and a piece of paper.

He nodded towards a small room behind the glass panel. 'Go through,' he said gruffly.

Topaz went through the door and into a tiny room, no bigger than a box—empty except for a microphone and a music stand on which she put her piece of paper. Again and again she tried to put on the headphones, but they kept slipping off her ears and down on to her cheeks. Behind the glass screen, she could see Tone rolling his eyes.

His bored voice boomed through into the room. 'Hold them over your ears.'

Topaz did as she was told and peered at the script.

To launch our new Oriental range, we're hammering down the price of all our products. Branches all over Starbridge.

Topaz thought of Octavia swanning off to be the burger girl.

That should be have been me! she thought angrily. *All I'm left with are two measly little lines!*

'Can we run through?' said Tone. 'I need to check your levels.'

A green light on the wall snapped on. Tone pointed his finger at Topaz and mouthed, 'GO!'

'To launch our new Oriental range, we're hammering down the price of all our products,' she growled. 'Branches throughout Starbridge.'

'You're supposed to be pleased at the thought of a new burger,' a different voice boomed over the intercom. 'Try and sound it.'

Julian Burbank had come into the studio.

Tone gave another signal for GO! and Topaz leant into the microphone.

This time, she'd try not to sound angry. It would help if she wasn't feeling so unwell all of a sudden.

'To launch our new Oriental range, we're hammering down the price of all our products,' said Topaz in a monotonous voice.

Julian slapped his forehead and leaned towards the glass panel before she'd even got to the second line.

'If you can't get into the feeling of the product, we'll have to get your friend back to do the voice-over *and* the advert,' he said. 'We can't waste any more time.'

Topaz felt stung. There was *no way* she would give Octavia the satisfaction of knowing she had been sacked from a voice-over. Octavia's voice-over! She remembered the advice Pearl Wong had given her in her first term when she'd told Topaz she'd been in a Speedy Snax advert.

'I felt the moment and smelt the moment!' she had said. 'That's what made my "Mmmm" so special.'

Topaz realized she had to make it sound as if the news about the new

Speedy Snax burgers was *the* most exciting news in the history of the fast food world, *however* she was feeling. It wasn't just a case of smelling the moment, it was a case of selling the moment.

'Sorry, Mr Burbank,' said Topaz. 'I'm ready to go again.'

'In that case, we'll go for a live one!' Julian boomed over the intercom. 'Let's try and make up some time!'

Tone started pulling levers and pushing buttons. Next to the green light, a red bulb burst into life and Tone gave the signal. Topaz pulled herself up straight, smiled into the microphone and said with an excited smile, 'To launch our new Oriental range, we're hammering down the price of ALL our products! Branches all over Starbridge!'

Tone came through the intercom.

'There's a rumbling noise on the playback,' he said. 'Can you go again?'

Topaz nodded and stepped up to the microphone. The red light snapped on

147

and just as Topaz opened her mouth, another low rumble went around the room. Then a gurgling sound as if a volcano was about to erupt.

'Cut!' shouted Tone. 'Is that *your* stomach rumbling?'

Topaz nodded. She'd been trying to ignore the fact that she felt unwell, but now she felt sick and dizzy. Her stomach churned and she felt beads of sweat begin to form on her forehead. She remembered the dodgy Duck Dippers.

'I'll be fine,' Topaz said, holding the microphone to steady herself. 'Let's go again.'

Tone adjusted the sound levels and called for a live recording. Topaz gulped. A true professional never let anyone down at the last minute. If people could go on stage with broken legs, she could stand in front of a microphone feeling sick. *Very* sick. She thought of the Precious Gems school motto: We Sparkle Whatever the Occasion. However she felt, the show *must* go on!

The red light glowed and Topaz

stepped forward to the microphone. She looked sick, she felt sick, but her voice was full of excited enthusiasm.

'To launch our new Oriental range, we're hammering down the price of ALL our products! Branches throughout Starbridge!'

Tone gave her a 'thumbs up' sign from behind the glass.

'Perfect!' shouted Julian over the intercom. 'You're a natural! Let's get another ten down to be sure.'

'Give me a moment!' gasped Topaz, clamping her hand over her mouth and running out of the studio.

CHAPTER THIRTEEN

The rest of the recording had been a nightmare. Tone found Topaz a bucket and said it was no problem and he could edit out any puking noises at the end of each take. He always had to do it for the Thrash Metal Monster Maniacs, he said, but in their case it was to do with one too many pints in the pub the night before, rather than a plate of dodgy dippers. Julian had suggested that if she felt too ill they find someone else for the voice-over, but Topaz hadn't come this far to be replaced, especially since he'd had told her what a natural she was.

'If you replace me I'll tell *everyone*

that it was Speedy Snax that made me ill!' she'd told Julian, surprised at how like Octavia she sounded.

Julian, worried that Health and Safety would find out that rotting Duck Dippers had been hanging around the studios for days, didn't argue. He even paid for a taxi to take her back to Andromeda Road, where she managed to climb the stairs to the top-floor flat and collapse into bed, only to have to get out again moments later to rush to the bathroom.

The doctor came and said that Topaz had food poisoning. Bad food poisoning.

'Can't you remember eating anything strange?' the doctor asked her.

Topaz shook her head. Even if she could admit to being at the Speedy Snax shoot, she didn't want to get Julian Burbank into trouble. She might need to work with him again.

The next morning Topaz's mother rang Precious Gems and said that

Topaz was still too ill to go to school.

'As there are only a few days left until the end of term I might keep her off for the rest of the week,' Lola had said.

Topaz lay slumped in bed and felt miserable. Her mum had brought the television into her room and though it burbled away in the background, she couldn't be bothered to watch it. She was missing the end of term and her mother was out of pocket as she'd had to pay someone to do her cleaning jobs so that she could look after her daughter. Topaz's legs still felt wobbly and she couldn't eat anything without her stomach churning. She'd gone behind Miss Diamond's back and *still* Octavia Quaver had got the lead role. There was still the risk she would lose her scholarship to Precious Gems— and what did she have to show for it? Two spoken lines in an advert she couldn't admit to and severe food poisoning. The consequences of suffering from bigus fibosis were much more severe than she had anticipated.

Topaz began to sob. Before, if she'd

been ill, Janice Stone would be round, telling her what she was missing—or texting her from lessons, telling her how lucky she was to be missing them. Her old friends at Starbridge High were no longer her friends and her new friends weren't the sort of friends her old friends used to be.

Topaz heard the buzzer go and the sound of footsteps on the steps up to the flats.

Her mother put her head around the door of the bedroom.

'You've got visitors!' she said, as Ruby and Sapphire peered from behind her mother's shoulders.

*   *   *

'I hope you don't mind,' said Ruby, 'but we got your address from Miss Diamond.'

'We looked up L'Amour in the phone book but there didn't seem to be any entries,' said Sapphire. 'You must be ex-directory. We are. Mum doesn't want the press or her fans calling her at home.'

153

Topaz said nothing. She hadn't told her friends that she had changed her name from Love to L'Amour because she thought it sound more glamorous and exactly the sort of thing stars did.

'Did you come on the bus?' she asked.

This time it was Sapphire's turn to go red and not say anything.

Ruby looked pleased. 'Sapphire's chauffeur brought us!' she said. 'He's waiting outside.'

Topaz's mouth fell open. 'You have a chauffeur?' she asked Sapphire, who shrugged, nodded and rolled her eyes all at the same time.

'Cool!' said Topaz.

'So,' said Ruby, 'what happened? The last we saw of you, you were off to the Speedy Snax shoot to tell them Pearl had fallen ill. The next thing we know, Miss Diamond says you're not coming back until next term.'

Topaz looked her friends straight in the eye. There had been too much lying going on. It was time to tell the truth.

'Bigus fibosis,' she said. 'I told the

Speedy Snax people that Pearl was suffering from bigus fibosis.'

Ruby and Sapphire looked blank for a moment and then Sapphire began to laugh. 'Big fibs!' she cried. 'You told them Pearl was suffering from big fibs!'

'And they believed you?' asked Ruby.

Topaz bristled. 'I'm a very good actress,' she said. 'I convinced them.'

'So who got Pearl's part?' asked Ruby.

Topaz wrinkled her nose and slumped even further down the bed. 'The Evil One.'

'Octavia Quaver?' asked Sapphire.

Topaz nodded. 'She was going to do the voice-over but they gave her Pearl's part instead.'

'So who got Octavia's part?' asked Ruby.

Even though Topaz buried herself under the blanket her eyes gave the answer away.

'No!' cried Sapphire. 'You didn't!'

And then, just as the Crispy Duck Dippers had done, it all came pouring out. How she'd really tried not to put herself forward for a part but that her mouth had a life of its own, and then she'd been offered Pearl's part but Pauline Quaver had put a stop to it because of Zit Stop!, so she'd done the voice-over but eaten old Duck Dippers and been sick. And all because of telling big fibs.

'How are you going to explain *that* to Miss Diamond?' asked Ruby. 'You know she'll pull your scholarship if she finds out.'

Topaz drew the blanket right up over her head and wailed, 'I know. Nothing can cheer me up.'

'Look!' Ruby shouted. 'Look at the TV!'

The girls watched in awe as the Speedy Snax logo popped on to the screen and on walked Octavia Quaver, her arms full of burgers and dippers and fries. But instead of tossing her blonde curls and gazing lovingly into the camera, smacking her lips at the thought of eating something from Speedy Snax, she was dressed as a giant burger in a bun, lettuce leaves on her feet and a wig made out of noodles topped with a hat resembling a slice of tomato.

An excited and very familiar voice rang out, 'To launch our new Oriental range, we're hammering down the price of ALL our products!' at which point a giant inflatable hammer appeared and bopped Octavia on the head, causing her to drop all the Speedy Snax products she was carrying. The camera zoomed in to a close up of Octavia looking shocked, whilst Topaz announced, 'Branches all over Starbridge!'

The girls stared open-mouthed at the television and then began to laugh and laugh until their sides ached and tears rolled down their cheeks.

Topaz forgot about feeling ill, leapt out of bed and danced around the bedroom singing, 'Octavia's a burger, Octavia's a burger.'

The girls couldn't wait until the next ad break to see whether Octavia appeared.

'Aren't you worried Miss Diamond is

going to find out?' asked Ruby.

Topaz shook her head. 'No one is going to recognize my voice,' she said. 'I bet even my mum doesn't know it's me.'

Ruby and Sapphire looked doubtful.

'I'll prove it to you,' said Topaz. 'Just wait.'

As the next ad break started Topaz shouted for her mum. Lola Love popped her head around the door.

'You look better,' she said. 'Something's cheered you up!'

'Come and see if Octavia is on,' said Topaz. 'The nasty one from Rhapsody's I've told you about. She's dressed in a burger costume!'

Sure enough, the Speedy Snax logo came on to the screen and Octavia walked on in her lettuce shoes and tomato hat. The girls rolled about on Topaz's bed, squealing with delight. If anything, the advert was funnier the more you saw it.

'What did you think, Mum?' Topaz asked. 'What did you think of Octavia?'

Lola looked puzzled. 'I couldn't really see what she looked like under all those noodles, but there was something *very* familiar about whoever did the voice-over.'

Topaz gulped. 'Familiar in what way?' she asked.

Lola shrugged. 'I'm not sure. I've definitely heard it somewhere before.'

The phone rang and Lola went into the hall to answer it. Through the open bedroom door the girls could hear her saying, 'Of course, Miss Diamond. I'll tell Topaz you'll need to see her as soon as she gets back to school next term.'

Ruby and Sapphire gasped. Topaz's heart began to race. She slumped back on the bed as beads of sweat began to glisten on her forehead. Miss D must have seen the advert after all! Why else would she be phoning? It was obvious that the *moment* Topaz went back to Precious Gems she would be expelled. She imagined herself walking through the gates of Starbridge High and Kylie Slate sneering at her. Her dreams of becoming a star would be shattered and she might never see Ruby and Sapphire again.

'You poor thing,' said Lola, coming back into the bedroom and seeing her daughter looking pale again. 'This bug has really taken it out of you. Never mind, by the end of the holidays you'll be better and ready to go back to Precious Gems. I bet you can't wait.'

Topaz nodded weakly and pulled up the bedclothes with shaking hands. One thing was certain. The start of next term at Precious Gems Stage School was going to be *very* interesting indeed!

Are you ready to Wok?

THE WOK & SPRING ROLL TAKEAWAY

ORIENTAL FOOD – FISH & CHIPS – CURRY SAUCE – PICKLED EGGS & GHERKINS

We wok around the clock!
Open 24 hours a day - 7 days a week - 365 Days a year

Corner of Galaxy Street & Stellar Terrace
T: Starbridge 478
Proprietor: Mr Wong

We Deliver! (occasionally)

Voted "Best Takeaway in Starbridge"
Cash only - No Credit cards or cheques

/// SPEEDY SNAX! ///

Clogging your arteries with grease - IN A FLASH!

Food for gourmands - not gourmets!

Fries with everything - including our speciality: Double Burger, Double Fries & Free Airline-Style Sick Bag!

BRANCHES THROUGHOUT THE COUNTRY